BURNING FOR CHRISTMAS

BURNING FOR THE BRAVEST

KAYE KENNEDY

DEDICATION

Grandma

Thanks for teaching me to love books, for being my #1 fan and cheerleader, and for always making Christmas special.

NOTE FROM THE AUTHOR

I can't thank you enough for choosing to read Keith and Brielle's love story. This book is a standalone, but it is set in the same world as my Burning for the Bravest Series, which features New York City firefighters who love hard and make love harder. A few of the characters from the series appear in this book and Keith makes an appearance in the series. You do not have to read the series before reading this, but if you enjoy this story, you'll adore the others as well.

If you're new to me, here's a fun fact: I was a firefighter in a previous chapter of my life, until an injury sustained in a house fire put an end to that. I was actually the third generation of firefighters in my family. I grew up with a father who is now an ex-chief, and I told myself that I would *never* date a firefighter... but then I fell in love with my lieutenant.

After seven years together, we parted ways, but I took away a plethora of knowledge about the inner workings of the FDNY (that's the New York City Fire Department). When I decided to start publishing, I knew I wanted to write from experience and that's how these stories came to be. Plus, the stereotype of firemen being sexy comes from somewhere, right? In my books, I stick as close to reality as possible, but I have used some creative freedom for the sake of the stories.

Note: Any parallels found here to actual people or places are purely coincidental, as this is a work of fiction. You may notice I refer to some places that actually exist, but what I say about them is purely my opinion and I don't stay completely true to reality.

Lastly, there is a subplot in this story regarding racism because the heroine is mixed race. While I come from a culturally diverse background, I am not a Person of Color; however, that does not mean I don't have a responsibility to use my voice to effect social change.

In the author community, there is sincere hesitation on the part of white authors when it comes to writing black characters. Admittedly, I am one of them. I went back and forth for quite a long time over whether I should just make Brielle white to avoid getting things wrong and upsetting readers, but that is the exact mindset that we as a society have a responsibility to change. We need to get comfortable with being uncomfortable. Despite being warned off by several authors, I had to stay true to my vision for Brielle's character and this story.

I had a diversity editor perform a sensitivity read on my manuscript prior to publication, simply to make sure I wasn't unintentionally offending anyone. While there are racist characters portrayed in this story, their viewpoints are not my own, rather they are viewpoints that I have observed as being problematic in our society. If it makes you uncomfortable, good, it's meant to; uneasiness breeds change.

I have my degrees in literature and my thesis was titled, *A Cross-Cultural Examination of Mother-Daughter Relationships in Ethnic American Literature.* I examined works that had Asian American, Native American, and African American characters. I say this because I dedicated years of my life solely to doing extensive research into how experiences in these cultures differ from my own, and I've drawn upon my academic background in my creation of this novel.

Cultural diversity has always been an interest of mine and as a long-time fan of the romance genre, I'm disheartened by the lack of diversity, which is why I feel obligated to use my platform as an author to change that.

Please note, that I have tried my best to create an authentic portrayal of life for someone who is mixed race, but I'm sure there will be people who feel I've gotten things wrong. To you, I apologize. Please know that I only have the best of intentions.

All that being said, race is not the main focus of this novel. This is a feel-good love story with an HEA and all the warmth of a Christmas tale.

Thank you for taking this journey with me and I hope you enjoy experiencing Keith and Brielle's journey to find love.

Hugs & Happily Ever Afters,

Kaye Kennedy

ONE

KEITH

My back strained as I heaved an extraordinarily large unconscious man through the living room of his apartment. I was sucking through the air in my SCBA bottle and I questioned whether I'd have enough to get me off the fire floor. At the rate I was going, I wondered if I'd even make it out of the dang apartment. I'd gone into the fire with Jace Palmer, one of the other guys on Ladder 64, but we'd come across a kid, so Palmer had left with the boy while I finished sweeping the apartment. That's when I'd located this big fella. At two-hundred pounds, I was no slouch, but this fucker easily had a buck-fifty on me. And he was dead weight, which only made him seem heavier.

I'd fastened a halo harness with my webbing to make it easier to drag the guy out, but it was still a challenge. A loud boom bellowed from the kitchen. We had to get out of there. Fast. I wasn't sticking around to find out what had been the source of the noise—it couldn't be anything good. I hooked my Halligan through the loops of the webbing in an attempt to use the steel bar for leverage. We inched through the apartment.

Panting, I bore down, digging in with my heels, and pulled. I simply needed enough momentum to keep us moving. I had chocked the apartment door open when we'd entered the unit and I could see the faint light in the hallway mere feet from me. From what I'd gathered, there was fire in two units, but it was also threatening to enter a third. We were the only Ladder company on scene and the other guys on my squad were all occupied, so I was on my own.

I finally got the victim to the door. Don't ask me why, but I'd half expected conditions to be better out in the hall. They weren't. My SCBA's vibe alert went off, causing my face piece to vibrate, telling me that I had maybe five minutes of air left. Under normal conditions, I could squeeze some more time out of it, but all attempts to control my breathing failed miserably.

Being a firefighter was the best dang career in the world. Except when it wasn't. Then, it was really fucking shitty. This was one of those times.

The salty taste of sweat dripping from my lip into my mouth made me thirsty and I tried to blink away the beads that fell from my brow into my eyes, but they stung nonetheless. My forearms screamed from the strain of the victim's weight as I hefted him, inch-by-inch down the carpeted hall. It couldn't be slick, slippery tile, right? No, it had to be carpet, which might as well have been Velcro. Like this wasn't hard enough. We were thirty feet from the stairwell, but it felt like three-hundred feet.

"You've got this, Keith. Don't be a pussy. Pull," I muttered to myself before gritting my teeth and tugging.

"Pull."

I tugged.

"Pull." The muscles in my neck tightened.

I tugged.

"Pulllllll."

My feet slipped out from under me and I landed on my ass.

"Fuck," I screamed. I was nearly out of air and my frustration level was nearly convincing me to leave the guy there. But I would never do that. No, I'd die trying to save him, but that didn't mean I was immune to thinking about taking the easy way out. All I had to do was get him into the stairwell, then we'd wait for my team to come up with a stair chair and we'd get him to safety as a crew.

I got back on my feet and heaved the bar again while grunting through my teeth. I was seriously regretting the thousand push ups I'd done earlier that afternoon. Dylan Hogan, one of the guys in my company, had challenged me to it. Said he didn't think I could do a thousand in thirty minutes. I'd proved him wrong and at twenty-nine-minutes and fifty-four seconds, I'd won myself twenty bucks, but I'd give up that twenty and then some to take back those push ups right about then.

I checked the gauge on my SCBA. It was well into the red zone and I wasn't gonna make it without running out of air, so I got on my radio. "This is Hart. I'm having a hell of a time getting a large victim out on the fire floor. Can I get some manpower up here with a stair chair? And bring me another bottle. I'm almost out of air."

"10-4, Hart," Captain Andrews acknowledged. "Hogan just got out here, I'll send him back up to you."

"10-4, Captain. If you can spare another body, too, I think we need it."

"I'll see what I can do."

I returned to dragging the guy down the hall. Three-quarters of the way to the stairs, my air ran out. I dropped the Halligan and reached for my regulator, twisting it off. Taking my chances with smoke inhalation was better than wearing a face-piece without airflow. I held my breath and prayed that Hogan would get there soon.

Gripping the Halligan, I got in one more solid tug before falling to the ground again. Like a fucking angel in hell, Hogan burst through the door followed closely by Palmer.

Palmer nudged me forward so he could access my SCBA and change out my empty bottle. Once it was screwed in, he said, "Good to go."

I snapped my regulator back into place and took in the best breath of air I'd ever had. I'd been on the job for three years and this was the first time I'd run out of air. Not something I needed to repeat. Ever.

"Fuck, bro. How far have you dragged this guy?" Hogan asked as he hauled the victim forward a few inches.

"Too...dang...far." I was still catching my breath from the exhaustion.

Palmer removed my Halligan from the harness loops and handed it to me. "Go get the chair ready. It's at the top of the stairs."

I didn't argue and made my way to the stairwell while Palmer and Hogan each took a loop and dragged the victim the rest of the way. Once at the stairs, we muscled the victim into the chair and strapped him in. By that point, we were all panting heavily. Hogan and Palmer gripped the handles at the foot of the chair so they'd take the brunt of the weight, while I held onto the handles by his head to stabilize the chair as we slid it down the three flights.

By the time we made it outside, I was ready to collapse. While the Engine charged through the door with the hose line, I took a much-deserved break. After chugging a bottle of water, I was feeling a bit better—just in time to go inside for overhaul.

OF COURSE, the call had come in half an hour before shift change. It never failed. Whenever I had somewhere to be after work, we always caught a late run. Someone had set their kitchen on fire while making dinner, which happened more often that you'd think. Once back at our firehouse on the Upper Westside of Manhattan, I rushed through a shower and headed out to meet my girlfriend, Megan.

I was two hours late by the time I got to her apartment. When I went to kiss her hello, she offered me her cheek and refused to make eye contact as she poured herself a glass of wine, not bothering to offer me one.

I settled into the armchair facing her in the open living space. "Sorry, Meg. I can't control when shit catches on fire."

"Language," she snapped.

"Sorry."

We'd been dating for six months so things were starting to get serious, but truth be told there was something missing that I couldn't quite put my finger on. Despite that, I wanted to make it work. Although I was only twenty-five, I was under some serious pressure to settle down. Being a fireman already made me the black sheep of the family, and I think my parents thought that if I got married, they'd be able to convince my wife to talk some sense into me and get me to enter politics before I was too old.

Megan was a lawyer and came from a prominent New York family, which made her perfect by my parents' standards. While they'd never met her, I knew she was exactly the kind of girl they'd want me to be with. My mother was a debutante and sat on the board of several charitable organizations. She came from old southern money. My father's a senator and former governor of Kentucky. There was a particular image we Hart's were expected to uphold. My older brother, Corbett, toed the line without hesitation. He was well on his way to following in our father's footsteps. Me on the other hand? Well, I'm a fireman. No need to say more.

Megan perched against her kitchen island sipping on a glass of Pinot Grigio while twirling a strand of blonde hair around her finger. "We missed our dinner reservation. I can probably get us into La Salle for dinner, but you need to change." She was dressed like she was going to dinner with the mayor. Her high-waisted black flare pants and satin mulberry purple button-down top were in stark contrast to what I was wearing.

I glanced down at my jeans and long sleeve tee that had my firehouse emblem over my heart. I was in no mood to get dressed up for the likes of La Salle. "Can we order in? I'm beat. That last run really took it out of me." My muscles were still burning.

She sighed. "What are we doing, Keith?"

I narrowed my eyes. "Not sure what you mean."

She placed her wine glass down on the counter. "I know that us dating is smart from a strategic standpoint, but we're so...different."

I sucked in my cheeks. "Where are you going with this?"

She crossed to the chair beside mine and took a seat. "We come from similar backgrounds. We should be a good match, but while I embrace where I came from, you seem to be running from it."

I rarely told anyone who my father was, but Megan had figured it out early on. I should've known then that she was only interested in me for my connections. "And you're getting this from me being too tired to go out to a fancy restaurant?" What she'd said hadn't been a lie, but still.

"Not just tonight, Keith." Her perfect French manicured nails rapped against the arm of the chair. "You're wasting your potential. You have your degree in political science from Columbia University, but you choose to breathe smoke for a living instead. I don't get it."

The only reason I had that degree was because my parents practically forced it on me. I folded my arms. "Where is this coming from?"

She shrugged. "I had a talk with my dad earlier. If I'm going to make partner in the firm by the time I'm thirty, I need to be with someone who matches my ambitions."

As exhausted as I was, I hopped to my feet. "Being a fireman doesn't mean I lack ambition. I'm studying for the lieutenants' exam. I want to work my way up. Make chief one day. You know that."

She nodded. "Yes, I know. But that goal doesn't line up with mine. I need someone who's going to want to get dressed up and go to La Salle with me. Networking is important, Keith, and I have an image to uphold."

That world didn't appeal to me in the slightest, but apparently Megan thought that's what she was getting by dating Senator Graham Hart's son.

I ran my hand over my smooth jaw. "You knew what I did when you met me."

"I did." She averted her eyes.

"But you thought you could get to my father through me and that'd be worth it."

She shook her head. "No—"

"Save it."

"I didn't care that you were a firefighter. But given how you grew up, I thought you'd be into the finer side of life like I am."

I scoffed. "The finer side? Honey, that life is full of backstabbers just waiting for you to step out of line. You might be fine with putting on a fake face, but I left that shit behind me."

She feigned offense.

"And, yes, I said shit. I curse. Get over it."

She smoothed her hands over the front of her blouse. "Well."

"I'm out. Have a good life, Megan."

She didn't bother to stop me as I went for the door.

Once outside, I tucked my hands into the pockets of my winter coat as light flurries fell onto the sidewalk around me. I probably should've been upset, but instead I was relieved. Dating Megan had been a lot of work. Sometimes I truly questioned my sanity when it came to my choice in women. For some reason, I always went for the type I'd grown up around, but it usually happened without my realizing it until it was too late.

Megan didn't live far from Times Square—right in the middle of the action. People buzzing with the holiday spirit weaved around me clutching shopping bags filled with gifts. Shop windows were adorned with glitter and garland and lights. New York truly was magical this time of year. My apartment was about a ten-minute walk and even though it was cold and my body was aching, I chose to hoof it. I figured taking that time would be good to clear my head.

My phone vibrated and I reached into my jeans to grab it. My mother's face was displayed on the screen. I swiped the green button and put it to my ear.

"Hello, Mother."

"Keith, darling, how are you?" Her proper southern accent was almost comical. It sounded like it came straight out of *Gone with the Wind*, but cross my heart it was genuine.

"Just fine. How are you? How's the Colonel?" My father had been a colonel in the Army before he entered politics. When we were kids, he had always insisted on being addressed by his rank. It was better than being expected to call him Senator.

"Oh, you know how hectic things get around here before our soirée."

Shit. I'd forgotten about the annual Christmas party that

my parents threw in D.C. before Congress broke for the holi-days. "Uh, right. I bet."

"I'm calling to find out when you and your girlfriend will be arriving. I simply cannot wait to meet her."

Double shit. "Yeah, about that—"

"Keith Percival Hart, do not tell me that you are not bringing that girl of yours because—"

"Relax. She's coming." I leaned up against a building to get out of the stream of pedestrians and pinched the bridge of my nose. "We'll be down there on Friday." My parents had made it abundantly clear over the years that I had to show up to the party with a respectable date for the sake of our family's image. They hadn't cared that every year I'd brought a different woman, as long as she had fit the mold.

"Oh, goody. I simply cannot wait to meet her."

"She can't wait to meet you either."

"You will be staying with us, yes?"

"No," it came out more sharply than I'd intended, so I took a breath. "I'll book us a room." Staying together with Megan under my parents' roof would be a nightmare.

Several voices streamed through the phone in the back-ground. My mother replied to them. "Yes, I will be right there." Then she addressed me, "Lovely, darling. Listen, I must go, but I will see you in a few days. Kiss kiss."

She hung up before I could say goodbye. I hesitated for a moment because I probably should've marched my way back to Megan's and groveled to get her to come to the party with me, but I didn't have the energy for that. Instead, I stepped away from the building and turned toward home. I'd call her the next day and convince her then. At the very least, she'd be thrilled at the prospect of furthering her career by rubbing elbows with senators. Then, when we got home, we could go our separate ways.

I was over this day. All I wanted to do was crawl into my bed and sleep. Pushing away the thought of having to endure a weekend rubbing elbows alongside my ex-girlfriend, I continued down the sidewalk. Each step bringing me closer to home and bringing an end to this supremely miserable day.

TWO

BRIELLE

After changing out of my work clothes and into a sweatshirt and leggings, I settled onto the gray leather couch—the soft and expensive kind, not the hard and squeaky kind—in an apartment that I'd never in a million years thought I'd be able to afford. Six months before, I'd lost my old apartment because my ex-roommate turned out to be a psycho bitch. Thankfully, my friend, Keith, had come to the rescue and had let me move in with him. I'd known him for a couple of years and I thought it might be weird living with a guy, but it wasn't. Actually, it was the opposite. Living together worked really well for us both.

I cradled my warm mug of chamomile tea, with my legs curled up beneath me, and reached for the remote before turning on the news channel. I was waiting for my mom's report on the embezzlement scandal involving the Prime Minister's Chief of Staff. She's a foreign correspondent for the Global News Network (GNN) with dual citizenship in the US and the UK. My father used to be a correspondent, too, but he had given it up and started teaching broadcast journalism at St. John's University in Queens, NY a few years ago, while I was in college. I'd grown up bouncing back and forth over the great, blue pond known as the Atlantic Ocean. When I had decided to go to college at Cornell University in Manhattan, my father had decided it was time for him to stop travelling. Realistically, he didn't want to leave me in America all by myself, but he'll never admit to that. Besides, he was thriving as a professor.

I took a sip of my tea and savored the warming sensation that flowed through my body. It was the beginning of December and winter had undoubtedly arrived. Snow flurried outside the floor-to-ceiling living room windows. I had the apartment to myself when Keith worked his two to three twenty-four hour shifts per week. And then there were the nights, like this one, when he stayed at Megan's. She was so wrong for him, but he was seemingly oblivious to it.

Since I've known Keith, he's had a few different girlfriends, and each was worse than the last. For a smart guy, he sure had awful taste in women. He could get anyone he wanted, yet he dated these high-maintenance hussies who didn't appreciate who he truly was. It was always the same story.

Mom's voice came through the television, distracting me from my tangent on Keith's poor choice in women. She was a real pro. My mom was one of those people who seemed born to be on camera. And she was beautiful. Her shoulder-length dark brown hair was always styled to perfection and her hazel eyes stood out against her beige skin. We looked a lot alike save for my brown eyes and darker skin tone, courtesy of my dad who's black. People often asked if we were sisters, which hopefully means I'll age just as gracefully as Mom has.

As Mom finished her report, the door knob turned. Before I could react to the pending intruder, Keith walked in. He dropped his keys in the bowl on the small glass table beside the door and hung his coat up in the front closet.

"Hey. I thought you were staying at Megan's tonight."

His mouth was turned down and his brows were furrowed.
Uh oh.

He sighed. "That's over." He kicked off his shoes before making his way across the oak wood floors and collapsing onto the other end of the couch.

"What happened?" I tried to sound surprised. I'd been anticipating this moment for weeks.

"It wasn't working. We've been trying to force our puzzle pieces together, but they simply don't fit. So I ended it."

"You ended it?" I asked, genuinely surprised. I would've put my money on Megan. She had seemed to have one foot out the door for a bit, while Keith seemed content to stick it out even if he hadn't been happy.

He hummed. "I think so. I mean, she was starting to break up with me, so I beat her to it."

I giggled. "Sorry."

He shrugged. "Yeah, I guess it is funny, huh? Oh well."

"Can I get you anything?"

He peered into my mug. "What are you having?"

"Chamomile tea. I can make you some."

He nodded. "Thanks."

I crossed the open living space to the kitchen and walked around the white quartz center island that matched the backsplash. Once at the pro-grade stainless steel stove, I checked the kettle and found there was enough water left, so I turned on one of the six burners to reheat it. After opening the cabinet above the espresso machine, I stretched to retrieve a mug, which I placed on the counter as I said to Keith, "You know you can do better than Megan, right?"

He sighed. "I guess."

"I'm serious." I grabbed the jar of chamomile and a tea strainer from the pantry, then filled the mesh metal ball with the fragrant yellow flowers.

"You never did like her," he responded with a smirk.

"Just looking out for you, roomie." The kettle began to whistle, so I poured the boiling water into the mug, then brought it back with me to the couch and handed it to Keith. "Here you go."

"Thanks." He took it and his large hands swallowed up the mug. "I should probably start letting you choose my girlfriends for me. You always seem to see what I can't."

I reached for my tea on the coffee table before settling back onto the couch. "You're a nice guy, Keith, and you look for the good in everyone, which is admirable. It's just that sometimes that makes you blind to the bad."

He brought the mug up to his red-flushed lips, still cold from being outside I assumed, and blew into the hot tea to cool it. "Well, I'm about to do a not-so-good thing."

I cocked my head. "Oh?"

"I have to go back to Megan and grovel so she'll go with me to my parents' Christmas party in D.C. this weekend."

My eyes narrowed. "Why on earth would you do that?"

"Because my mother is expecting me to bring my girlfriend and I'm not likely to find myself a new one of those in three days."

I put my tea on the coffee table, then tucked my legs up beneath me and faced Keith. "Hold up. So you're going to ask the girl you just broke up with to go away with you for a weekend with your family and just act like you're still together?"

He rubbed his chin.

"And you expect her to be on her best behavior after you broke up with her?"

"What other choice do I have?"

"Go alone. Literally, anything else besides what you're planning."

"Going alone isn't an option."

"Then find another date. You're," I paused to try and come up with the best way to tell my strictly platonic roommate what I thought of him, "you. That shouldn't be so difficult."

"Are you saying I'm a catch, Elle?" he teased. He was the only one who called me that. If friends ever shortened my name, it was to Bri. I kind of liked that I was Elle to him only.

I rolled my eyes. "Not like it's a secret."

"I'm afraid it's not as easy as you may think. My parents are..." His face twisted. Keith was relatively tight lipped when it came to his family. I knew he came from money and his father was an Army Colonel who split his time between Kentucky and D.C., while his mother was into charity work of some sort, but that was the extent of my knowledge. He hadn't ever wanted to divulge, so I'd never pushed.

He sighed. "They have these standards. I can't just show up with some chick I picked up in a bar."

"Oh, but you can live with one?" I jested.

He laughed. "Not the same. Besides I didn't pick you up."

"Not technically, no, but you still kind of did."

"You wish." He gave me one of his panty-melting smiles.

I punched him playfully in the arm. "Dream on."

The night Keith and I had met, I'd been out with a girl-friend. While she was in the bathroom, some incredibly inebriated guy had cornered me and said, *"You're beautiful. I'm going to kiss you now."*

Before I could knee him in the nuts, Keith had strolled over and put his arm around me. He'd said, *"There you are, baby. I've been looking for you,"* as he led me away from the creeper and over to an open area of the bar. Once in the clear, he'd said, *"Looked like you needed some help. Hope that was cool."*

"Yes, very much so. Thanks," I'd replied. I had been more than okay with pretending like I was Keith's *baby*, especially

because he looked like a Greek god. The first thing I had noticed about him was his bone structure. He's got a pronounced brow, prominent cheekbones, a strong jaw, and a square chin. All of that makes for one very striking man. Factor in his broad shoulders, his solid chest, his rippling biceps, his defined waist, and his six-foot-two frame and you get one heck of a specimen for the male species. And he has the slightest hint of a southern accent (but it really comes out when he's tired or he's been drinking). Needless to say, my lady parts had tingled when I'd first laid eyes on Keith Hart.

My bubble had been burst fairly quickly though because his actual girlfriend had arrived. I mean, of course, he had a girlfriend. I'd swallowed my disappointment and we all ended up hanging out together. Keith and I had slipped straight into the friend zone.

Keith took a sip of his tea. "I really don't see any other way around taking Megan."

I sighed. "There's got to be someone else you can take."

"I can't pull a girlfriend out of thin air."

"It doesn't have to be a girlfriend."

"Yes, it does."

"Why?"

His lips narrowed into a thin line. "Because my parents have made it clear that it's important for our family image for my brother and I to be dating 'respectable' women."

I huffed. "Well then Megan is definitely out."

We shared a laugh and then he said, "Seriously though. She fits the mold." The few times Keith had talked about his family had been very telling. It was apparent that he desperately wanted their approval for some reason. Why? I have no clue, but it was important to him and it wasn't my place to argue with his twisted logic.

"Why don't you just find someone who can *pretend* to be

your girlfriend? If you make it worth her while, I'm sure she'll even pretend to be whoever you want her to be. That way she fits the mold."

He tapped his fingers against his mug. "That's actually not a terrible idea."

"I have my moments." I winked.

His copper eyes stared at me a little too hard for a little too long.

"What?" I asked.

He put his mug down on the table. "What are you doing this weekend?"

I laughed. "I didn't mean take me."

"Why not? They've never met you, so they won't know."

Oh, he was serious? "You want *me* to pretend to be your girlfriend? I don't know if that's a good idea."

He put his hands together like he was praying. "Come on, please."

"But we're friends."

"Exactly why you're the perfect person to take. We know a lot about each other, so we could totally pull this off. Hell, you know more about me than Megan did. Plus, you fit the mold."

I puffed out my cheeks and slowly deflated them.

"Do me a solid here. I'll owe you one." The desperation in his tone tugged at my insides.

I grabbed my mug and finished the last sip of my cold tea, then I stared into the empty mug and took a breath before putting it back onto the table. I saw the hope in his eyes and chose to ignore the nagging voice in my head that was telling me that this was a bad idea. "Fine. But I will be collecting on that favor eventually because you're going to owe me a big one."

He leapt across the cushion, wrapping me in his arms, and tackling me into the armrest. "Thank you. Thank you. Thank you. You're the best, Elle."

I couldn't help but laugh. "Yeah, I am. Now let go of me so I can breathe."

He released me and sat back, allowing me up. "I seriously owe you."

I nodded. "I won't let you forget it."

He chuckled. "I'm sure you won't."

"Can you tell me what I just signed up for?"

"We'll leave for D.C. on Friday once you're finished with work. I'll get us two hotel rooms. The party is on Saturday at my parents' house. Then, we'll leave on Sunday to come home."

"All right. I can do that."

"Oh, and it's formal so I'll give you money to go get a dress."

"I get a fancy dress out of this? Next time, lead with that. I would've agreed much sooner."

He grinned. "I'll keep that in mind." He mimed like he was licking the tip of an old pen and then wrote in the air with it. "Elle can be bought with clothes."

I laughed. "Not just any clothes. High fashion, though, will always be a yes."

"Noted." He flashed me a smile that made his eyes sparkle.

KEITH ARRIVED at the studio early to pick me up for the weekend trip. I was an anchor for the US Broadcasting Company's (USBC) News at Noon. Being around my parents work so much when I was younger had given me the broadcasting bug. I always thought I'd follow in their footsteps and become a correspondent, but turns out I loved being an anchor.

During a commercial break I waved at Keith, who had snuck in during the broadcast. He smiled and gave me two thumbs up. He'd never been in the studio while I was on live before. Once we'd wrapped, I hastened to finish up the last of my work, then I met up with Keith and we headed out to his Range Rover. I'd packed my bags the night before and had left them by the door for Keith to grab before picking me up, so we could head straight to D.C.

Keith was unusually quiet and while we were in the Lincoln Tunnel, I asked, "You all right?"

He nodded, but his body language told me otherwise. I noticed how hard he was gripping the steering wheel and his jaw was clenched.

"Don't lie to me, Hart."

He huffed a few breaths. "Seeing my family stresses me out."

"I see that. Want to talk about it?"

"No." He sighed. "But I have to tell you something."

My curiosity piqued. "Okay."

"I haven't told you the full truth about who my father is."

I cocked my head. "So he's not an Army Colonel?"

"He is. But there's more." He shifted in his seat while his fingers tapped on the wheel.

I hated seeing him so worked up. Keith was usually so chill. Almost too chill sometimes. This anxiety was unusual for him.

"My father was the governor of Kentucky for eight years until my junior year of high school."

My eyebrows shot up and a chill crawled up my spine. A politician. "Oh?" I tried to sound calmer than I felt.

"And now he's a senator."

My blood ran cold. I swallowed. "A senator?"

"This party is for his cronies in Congress. It's one last hurrah before they break for the holidays and head back to their respective home states."

An entire party of politicians. Shoot me. I'd assumed that Keith's dad was some kind of advisor given his military background and the fact that he worked in D.C. sometimes, but I hadn't expected this. If I'd known about his political career, I never would've agreed to go. Not after what Mitchell, my ex, had done to me. He'd used me to impress the mayor of New York City—the *black* mayor—because he'd wanted a job working in his office. Mitchell had thought dating a girl who was mixed race would help his odds. When I'd found out, I'd broken up with him, but he'd already been hired at that point. Needless to say, I wanted nothing to do with politicians ever again.

My mouth was dry and I reached for my water bottle in the cup holder. It took longer than it should've for me to unscrew the cap because of how badly my hands were shaking.

Keith must've noticed because he said, "Don't be nervous. You're going to be great with them."

I swallowed half the bottle of water in one shot before replacing the cap. "You should've told me."

"I don't like to talk about it. I came to New York to escape that life. Here I can be anyone other than Senator Graham Hart's son." His voice dipped. "The Colonel's greatest disappointment."

I reached across the center and put my hand on his thigh. "How can you be a disappointment? You're a real-life hero. I'm sure your father is proud of you."

He sniggered. "Not even close. He expects me to go into politics. According to him, that's the only respectable career choice. My brother, Corbett, is following suit. The Colonel's waiting for me to do the same." He sighed. "He has his sights set on the presidency and he wants both of his sons to portray the right image for that to happen. That's why I couldn't take just anyone with me this weekend."

I gulped down the lump in my throat. I had an entirely new perspective on Keith. A lot of things made sense after this revelation. I was suddenly grateful that I hadn't decided to change into more comfortable clothes after my broadcast and that I'd stayed in my long sleeve, hunter-green, knit dress that fell to my knees. Keith needed me to make a good first impression on his family. Forcing myself to push aside my own uneasiness, I tried to soothe him. "That's ridiculous. You know that, right?"

He didn't respond.

I squeezed his thigh. "What you do as a firefighter is more admirable than any political career."

"I wish it were that simple, Elle. And I'm sorry I haven't told you before now, but like I said, it's a part of me that I'd rather forget about."

"Don't fret. I totally understand." I removed my hand from his leg. "But if your dad disrespects you in front of me, I can't promise to play nice."

That got a small laugh out of him. "Thank you for coming with me. Now that I think about it, there's honestly no other person I'd want to go with. You're a really great friend, Elle."

My heart squeezed. "Happy to do it." Especially knowing what the deal was. I'd imagine Megan would've made the whole trip about furthering her own career, and Keith would've had to go into the wolves' den without anyone having his back. I'd put aside my own hang ups about the compromised morals that went hand-in-hand with a political mindset because my friend needed me.

I'd been waiting a long time to be able to help Keith like he'd helped me. And I wouldn't let him down.

KEITH

We pulled up to my parents' place in Georgetown, which was the most desirable neighborhood in D.C., meaning it was also the most expensive. My mother would have it no other way. Their place was a three-story corner row house, complete with a wine cellar and a prized rose garden. The four-thousand square foot home boasted four bedrooms, each with its own bathroom, plus a powder room on the main level. At over two-million-dollars, it was opulence at its finest.

I parked my Range Rover on the street out front, directly behind my brother's. We'd each gotten one on our twenty-first birthdays. I still had the same one, but my brother was on his third. Granted, he was four years older than me and he lived in the D.C. area, so he used his car far more frequently than I did living in Manhattan. Besides, Corbett had been promoted earlier that year to the position of Legislative Director in our father's office, so he needed shiny new things. Appearances and all that.

I took a long breath. "Ready?" I asked Brielle, although I was asking myself just as much as I was asking her.

"Let's do it." She opened her car door before I could get out and do it for her.

I met her on the sidewalk and held my arm out for her to take. She hooked her fingers into the crook of my elbow. The sun had set half an hour before, and the Christmas lights lit up the block with the spirit of the holidays, making me smile. After all those years in the Governor's Mansion, I'd come to love the lavishness of decorations this time of year.

We passed through the iron gate and I lead Brielle up the steps to the oversized double doors, both of which were adorned with giant pine wreaths finished with red bows. Even though I had lived in this house and had my own key, I didn't feel right letting myself in, so I rang the doorbell.

Arina, my parents' housekeeper opened it. Her blonde hair was pulled into a French braid. In her Russian accent, she said, "Mr. Keith, so nice to see you." It didn't matter how many times I'd asked her to simply call me Keith over the years, she refused to drop the mister.

"Good to see you, too, Arina. This is Brielle."

She did a small curtsey. "Pleasure to meet you, Ms. Brielle."

"Likewise, Arina."

Arina stepped aside. "Please come. Senator and Mrs. Hart are in the sitting room with Mr. Corbett and Ms. Caroline." She took our coats and hung them in the closet.

"Thank you."

Brielle took my arm again as I lead her down the hall to the informal living room. But, let's be real, with my mother there was nothing informal about it.

The house was draped in twinkly white lights and I could hear the catering staff banging around in the kitchen prepping for the party the next day. As we entered the cozy room in the back of the house that lead to the outdoor patio and the garden, my mother rose to her feet. Her ash brown hair was styled in her signature chignon and she had on a full face of makeup. Lemon Hart was never seen without makeup. When I was younger, I'd often wondered if she'd slept with it on. Any age lines that the makeup didn't cover had been erased by Botox injections.

She smoothed out the creases in her black pencil skirt. "Keith, darling, you finally made it."

We were thirty minutes behind schedule and I knew she wouldn't let it slide. "Hello, mother."

My father, brother, and sister-in law all stood as well.

"Everyone, this is Brielle Jackson."

Her fingers tightened around my arm. "Thank you for having me. Your home is lovely."

"It is our pleasure, sugar," my mother replied.

I dropped my arm and Brielle let go so that I could give my mother and Caroline a hug. Then I shook Corbett's hand and the Colonel's while Brielle made her rounds being greeted. We took seats on the cream-colored sectional, opposite my brother and his wife, while my parents returned to their seats in the armchairs adjacent to the lit fireplace. Stockings hung on the mantle which was draped with fresh garland and dotted with candles. The whole house smelled of pine and cinnamon. It was comforting.

All eyes were on me and Brielle. I put my arm around her shoulders. *Let the inquisition begin.*

My father spoke first. "Ms. Jackson, tell us, what do you do?" He always looked the same. A man of large stature with hair in a neat crew cut, although it had nearly turned all gray.

"Please, Senator, call me Brielle."

My father bobbed his smooth chin.

"I'm an anchor for USBC News in New York."

The Colonel's brows arched, and my mother's already

perfect posture straightened even further. He responded, "That's impressive for someone so young."

"Thank you, Senator."

No way I was going to let Brielle get away with being so humble. "She earned it. Brielle won an Associated Press Award for a broadcast she did on gang violence in Brooklyn last year. The network was smart enough to promote her to an anchor slot after that. She's the youngest anchor the network has ever had."

"Congratulations. You should be very proud." The Colonel's smile looked genuine. It wasn't the fake kind he put on for the cameras and his constituents. *Hmm.*

Mother cut in. "Your parents must be quite proud of you, too, sugar. What do they do?" And the inquisition continued. Leave it to my mother to find out what kind of family my date came from within the first few minutes.

"Yes, they are. My mother is a foreign correspondent for GNN and my father used to be as well, but he retired from that life six years ago. Now he's a journalism professor at St. John's University."

Both of my parents beamed. It had never dawned on me before, but on paper, Brielle was exactly the kind of woman my parents would want me to be with. Lucky for me, she was as down-to-earth as they came, unlike my exes.

Friends, Keith. You and Elle are fake dating. Right.

Mother asked, "That is lovely. You come by your talents honestly. What are their names? Perhaps we have heard of them."

"Kimberly and Douglas Jackson."

My mother hummed. "We will have to look them up and see if we have ever crossed paths. Being in the public eye and all." She gestured toward Caroline. "My daughter-in-law is in the journalism world, too. She is the Assistant Press Secretary for Senator Jansen."

Brielle turned to Caroline. "Is that so?"

She nodded. "I have my degree in communications and public relations from Georgetown University. That's where Corbett and I met."

My brother asked, "How did you two meet?"

We'd gone over our story in the car. Brielle responded, "I was on scene reporting at a fire by Lincoln Center. Keith was there and I managed to wrangle him for an interview. We clicked and became instant friends. At the time, he had a girlfriend, and then I had a boyfriend, so it took a couple of years for us both to be single at the same time, but here we are."

The women swooned and the men nodded with approval. Brielle had suggested the story saying that a meet-cute like that would win everyone over. Whatever that meant, I guess she was right.

And then my father ruined the moment. "Glad to hear something good has come out of our son's *job*." The disdain in his voice was unmistakable. I was used to it. At least, Brielle seemed to have his approval.

I felt her stiffen beneath my arm. She had never been known to hold her tongue, so I squeezed her shoulders to keep her from snapping back.

She turned to look at me and gave me a smile as if to say, *I've got this*. Then she replied, "So many wonderful things have transpired because of Keith's *career*. Just the other night, he saved a man's life in an apartment fire. He's a hero. You've raised a wonderful son and I'm sure you're all incredibly proud of him. I know I am." Then she turned up and kissed me on the cheek.

I grinned. She was good. It was a slap disguised as a compliment. And dang she had soft lips.

Mother's constituents smile made an appearance. "Of course."

The subject shifted to discussing my brother and his role on my father's political team. I mostly tuned it out. At some point, Arina brought us each some red wine from my parents' cellar stash. While I snubbed my nose at a lot of the pretention, I'd always appreciate the fine wines. Caroline declined the offer and we all eyed her curiously.

Corbett stood up. "I suppose this is good a time as any. Caroline and I are expecting."

Mother performed a series of rapid mini claps. "Good heavens, this is wonderful news. Positively wonderful." She embraced Corbett and Caroline in succession, then dabbed at her eyes.

The Colonel wasn't a hugger, so he patted them both on the back. "Outstanding. Congratulations."

They'd been married four years, so it wasn't that much of a shock. Our parents had been pestering them for grandchildren since they'd returned from their honeymoon. I hugged them both, as did Brielle. Then I asked, "When are you due?"

Caroline smiled and held a hand over her stomach. "May twenty-ninth." Her tiny baby bump was barely visible beneath her loose black sweater.

I was going to be an uncle. That was fucking cool. Corbett and I were very different—always had been. As kids, I'd been into climbing all of the trees on our property and playing baseball with the neighborhood, while Corbett had preferred board games like Risk and Trivial Pursuit and watching painfully boring war documentaries. Despite our differences, I still loved him. And I'd love my niece or nephew, too.

The Colonel asked, "Can we announce this good news to our constituents? I'm certain they will be overjoyed to hear of the new addition to the Hart family."

I was surprised it had taken him a whole minute to ask.

Caroline chewed her lip and scrunched her eyes up at Corbett, a look that told me she wasn't comfortable with the idea, but my brother ignored it. "Of course," he said.

Caroline stiffened.

Corbett continued, "I think we can all agree it's perfect news to deliver for the holidays."

My sister-in-law's jaw clenched.

"Excellent. We can tell everyone tomorrow." My father pulled out his phone, no doubt contacting his Press Secretary.

Caroline chimed in. "Actually, I'd really like to wait a few more weeks. I haven't told Senator Jansen yet and I want him to hear it from me."

The Colonel waved her off. "Not a problem. There's plenty of time for you to speak to him before the party tomorrow."

"It is a soirée, Graham. Not a party," Mother corrected.

"Yes, yes. There's plenty of time for you to speak to Senator Jansen before the *soirée* tomorrow."

Caroline nodded. "Certainly, Senator."

I felt for her. We'd all been forced into things by my father at some point. Still, I couldn't keep quiet about this one. "Colonel, what's the rush? Give Caroline a week or so to sort it out on her end."

He looked up from his phone and stared at me with those penetrating copper eyes. He didn't say a word. Not backing down, I returned his gaze.

In my periphery, I noticed Corbett wrap his arm around Caroline. "It's not a big deal. We can announce tomorrow."

My father broke eye contact. "Good. My team will take care of everything."

My nostrils flared. Brielle placed her hand on my shoulder, calling for my attention. I glanced down at her and her presence instantly calmed me. She mouthed, *leave it.*

I took a breath and nodded. "We're going to head to the hotel. It's been a long day."

Mother fingered the strand of pearls around her neck. "I thought you were staying here?"

"No, I told you the other night on the phone that we were going to stay in a hotel."

"Nonsense. Cancel the hotel. Arina already made up your room. You will stay here."

"Mother, we're staying in a hotel," I snapped.

Her back straightened and her head slowly tilted to the side. "Is there a reason why you cannot stay here?" Suspicion laced her voice.

Fuck. I attempted to cover. "Brielle has just met you all. I think she'd be more comfortable in a hotel."

Mother's lips narrowed into a thin, straight line. Her attention turned to Brielle. "Is that true, sugar?"

Brielle hooked her arm around mine and responded to me directly. "I'm fine with staying here, babe."

I sucked in my cheeks and nodded. "I'll go get our bags."

The Colonel held up his hand. "Not necessary. Geoffrey will retrieve them."

As though the butler had sensed he was being summoned, he appeared in the doorway. In his British accent, he said, "Pardon my interruption. Mrs. Hart, the caterers have a menu question that they'd like to run by you in regards to tomorrow's soirée."

My mother excused herself and my father instructed, "Geoffrey, please retrieve the suitcases from my son's car and bring them up to his room."

"With pleasure, Senator." He turned to me. "May I have your keys?"

I handed them to him. "Thank you, Geoffrey."

He bowed his head and then made his exit right before

Arina entered. "Since the kitchen will be occupied all evening, would you like me to place a dinner order for the family, Senator?"

"That is a question best directed to Mrs. Hart."

"My apologies. I asked you since Mrs. Hart is occupied with the caterers. You like dinner precisely at seven and I'll need to place an order now to stay on schedule."

The Colonel nodded. "Very well. Yes, get us steaks from Morton's."

There was no way I was subjecting Brielle to a family dinner. Our little cocktail hour had been bad enough. Thinking on my feet, I blurted out, "Actually, Colonel, I promised to take Brielle out for a proper date. She's never seen D.C. this time of year and since we'll be busy with the party tomorrow, tonight's our only option."

He pointed his chin in my direction, those copper eyes assessing my motives no doubt. After a long breath, he said. "Very well." He smiled at Brielle. "This city is stunning during the holidays."

One bullet dodged.

"Will you be dining with us?" he addressed Corbett.

"Absolutely, Colonel."

While my father gave instructions to Arina, Geoffrey returned with my keys. I wasn't waiting a moment longer to get out of there. Especially since we were stuck spending the night. We said our goodbyes and I told the Colonel to let Mother know we'd see her later since she seemed busy with the caterers, then I practically dragged Brielle out the door.

As soon as we were on the front steps with the door closed behind us, I said, "I am so sorry."

Brielle laughed. "You owe me double for this one."

I didn't argue. "Deal."

I opened the car door for her and waited for her to get in

before I closed it, then made my way around to the driver's side. Wasting no time, I got the heat started and turned on the seat warmers.

"What would you like for dinner?" I asked.

She shrugged. "Something delicious."

Smiling, I eased away from the curb and took us toward the Potomac River. "You sure you're all right with sleeping here tonight?"

"It's fine. Your mother sounded suspicious. Better to make her happy than argue about it."

I sighed. "Yeah, that was probably the right call. But I'd told her the other day that I was staying in a hotel. She pulls this shit on purpose. Always needs to get her way."

I dialed the hotel on my car phone and cancelled our reservations. Since I'd booked the rooms under our family's extensive rewards account, they gave me a full refund. Sometimes, my family name came in handy. We pulled up to Bluegrass Barbeque a couple of minutes later and by some miracle, I managed to find a parking spot right on M Street not far from the big Christmas tree.

"Ready?" I asked as I reached into my coat to remove my tie before tossing it into the backseat.

Brielle nodded and we got out into the bustle of the city. The ornate street lights were adorned with wreaths and red bows. White strands of light looped over-head and wrapped around tree trunks while glowing snowflakes adorned buildings.

"Barbeque good with you?"

"Sure," she replied with a shiver. Her dress, while knit, likely didn't do much to keep her warm. Hopefully her knee-high leather boots helped some. I probably should've let her change before we'd left the house, but I'd been eager to get out of there, so I hadn't been thinking clearly. Besides, she looked good in that dress. Really good. Not that I thought about her in *that* way. Brielle and I were friends. That's all.

I offered her my arm so I could hold her close to keep her warm. She took it and followed me to the restaurant. Being that it was a Friday night during the holiday season, the place was packed. I put our name on the waitlist and gave the hostess my phone number to call me when our table was ready...in forty-five minutes to an hour.

I lead us back out to the street. "Sorry, Elle. I should've thought ahead and made us reservations for tonight when I booked the hotel rooms, but I hadn't been thinking about dinner." We probably would've eaten with my family if they hadn't managed to get on my nerves so quickly.

"Not a big deal." She squeezed my arm with her gloved hand as we walked down the sidewalk. "What should we do while we wait?"

"I've got an idea." I lead her to Georgetown Park Plaza where several light art installations were on exhibit. "We're here during Georgetown GLOW, which is an annual art exhibit featuring lighted installations created by artists from around the world."

"Wow, this is spectacular," Brielle commented as she gazed up at the multi-colored pompoms strung above the plaza walkway.

I had to agree with her, while not exactly Christmasy, they were festive in their own right. I pulled out my phone. "Let's take a picture." I angled the lens down so that the lights above us would be in the shot.

"Good idea. It'll help us sell us being a couple if we have photos to show off." Brielle leaned her head against my shoulder and I snapped the photo. That hadn't been why I wanted to take the picture—I thought it would be a cool shot with all the lights—but she was probably right.

"Are you freezing or are you up for a walk to the waterfront to see more lights?"

She hugged my arm and said, "Both," which made me laugh.

We walked through what the artist was calling an urban field. Long crystalline stems, designed to mimic wheat in a field, lit up the walkway. They had a magical feel to them, and we paused for another photo amongst the lights.

It took us a few minutes to get to the waterfront where there was a large ice-skating rink, another installation on exhibit, and the decorated boats in the harbor. Brielle's face beamed at the sight. "Totally worth being cold."

"Impressive, right?"

She nodded. "Very."

We took another photo by the large prisms that had an iridescent effect in various colors, before making our way along the river to admire the boats decked out in Christmas lights. Some even had inflatable Santas, reindeer, and snowmen on board.

"Do people always decorate their boats for Chirstmas?"

I nodded. "There's a boat parade of lights on the river every year."

She grinned. "How fun."

During the walk back to the restaurant, we took our time admiring all of the holiday window displays. Brielle squeezed my arm and pulled me over to a clothing store that had a display of toy soldiers. "I played Clara in my company's production of *The Nutcracker* while I was in high school."

"I bet you were amazing."

She gave me a playful smile. "I was."

I laughed. "I wish I knew you when you danced. I would've like to have seen you perform."

She sighed. "It feels like a lifetime ago." She pulled me

away and we kept moving down the sidewalk. "Some of these window displays are quite elaborate."

"Many of the small businesses here compete in the Holiday Window Art Competition and they spare no expense with their decorations."

"No kidding. It's not quite like Manhattan, but still beautiful."

By the time we returned to the restaurant, I couldn't tell which one of us had the bigger smile. There was something about the holiday spirit that simply made everyone happy.

We arrived as my phone rang. It was the hostess saying that our table was ready. I opened the door for Brielle and she released my arm as we went inside. Once at our table, we shed our layers. Well, she did. I'd only worn a coat. I couldn't be bothered with gloves, a scarf, and a hat. Way too much work. Besides, I tended to run hot.

Brielle opened the menu and laughed.

"What is it?"

"We come to D.C. for you to take me to a Kentucky barbeque joint."

I shrugged. "I'm a southern boy at heart. When we first moved here after my dad was elected, this quickly became my favorite restaurant. It reminded me of being back home in the Bluegrass State." The whole place had a country feel to it, from the music to the rustic décor. And the smell of smoked meat and brown sugar made it a slice of home. I unbuttoned my cuffs and rolled my sleeves up to my elbows.

The server came over with a basket of cornbread and we both ordered ribs and a beer. One thing I loved about Brielle was that she was never shy about eating like a lot of girls were. When our drinks arrived, I held mine up to cheers her. "To surviving a weekend with my family and a shit load of stuffy politicians."

While she clinked my glass, I couldn't help but notice her wince.

"What's wrong?"

She shook her head. "Nothing."

"I know my family can be a lot. Sorry if they made you uncomfortable."

She took a sip from her pint. "No big deal. But I've got to ask: were you adopted?"

A laugh escaped from deep within me. "Seems like it sometimes, but no I'm not."

"Those people are your polar opposites."

"That's a fair assessment."

Her blush-polished nails tapped on the wooden table. "They're not what I'd imagined. They're all a bit," she paused and puckered her lips, "a bit stuffy."

I laughed again. "Yeah, they are."

"And you're so chill."

I winked. "Thanks, Elle."

"Seriously. I mean your mother is named after a fruit," she declared with a giggle and I joined her.

"Lemon is a traditional southern name."

"And you have a butler. An actual *British* butler."

"Correction: my parents have a butler."

She shook her head. "Who are you, Keith Hart?"

"I'm still the same guy you know and love. But now you see why I keep quiet about my background. I'm not one of them. Never really have been."

She reached for a piece of cornbread. "Your brother fits right in, though."

I nodded and reached for a piece of the warm bread as well. "Corbett thrives in that environment while I've always been the rebellious one."

"Thank goodness for that." She took a bite.

"You're not into stuffy politicians?"

She scoffed and furrowed her brows. After swallowing the bread, she replied, "Definitely not."

There was a story there but before I could ask, our dinner arrived and the moment was lost as the server explained the flavors of all twelve sauces on our table.

"I meant to tell you earlier, but it was cool seeing you live in the studio today. You're pretty dang impressive, Elle." I watched her show on TV pretty much every day, but it was a totally different experience seeing her work live.

"Thanks," she uttered through a bashful grin before picking up a rib and nibbling on the bone.

Brielle was a stunning woman. I'd always thought so. Her latte-toned skin made her dark, round eyes stand out beneath her long, full lashes in the best way. She had the kind of eyes that could make a man feel thoroughly fucked with one glance. Not that I'd been the target of those sultry looks, but I'd seen her give them to other guys before. Had to admit, I'd always been a little jealous of those men. I'd often wondered if she and I would've dated if things had been different back when we met, but that ship had sailed. She was one of my best friends—end of story.

Brielle licked barbeque sauce off her finger. "You going to keep staring at me or do you plan on eating, too?"

I laughed as I picked up a rib. She was cute as hell chomping on barbequed ribs with her flawless camera-ready makeup and her perfectly styled, long, rich, dark-chocolate hair hanging over her shoulders in loose curls.

After dinner, we stopped at a café to get some tea. Brielle always ended her nights with a cup of tea. Usually, chamomile, but sometimes she'd go for mint or a decaf chai. Since we'd been living together, she'd gotten me into the habit as well. I'd never been a tea person before. Well, unless you count southern sweet tea, but Brielle had opened my palate to the different varieties, and I had to admit it helped me relax before bed.

Teas in hand, we got back in my car and I reluctantly drove us to the house. This time I used my key because I hoped my parents would be in bed and I didn't want to alert them to the fact that we'd returned. Once inside, I took Brielle's coat and hung it in the closet with mine before motioning for her to follow me upstairs. My room was on the second floor and when I got to the doorway I froze. I'd failed to consider the fact that there was only one bed.

I turned to her and whispered, "I can sleep in Corbett's old room."

She shook her head. "Wouldn't that make your parents suspicious?"

She had me again. Brielle brushed past and entered my bedroom.

I followed and shut the door. "I'll sleep on the floor."

"Don't be ridiculous."

"You sure?"

She nodded. "I wouldn't be able to sleep knowing you're curled up on the carpet."

I pointed to the attached bathroom. "You can use it first."

"Thanks." She snatched up her classic Louis Vuitton weekender bag, which had been a present from her parents when she'd made anchor, and disappeared into the bathroom.

I typically slept in my boxer briefs, but that wasn't an option, so I needed to find some shorts because I hadn't packed any. I went over to the walnut Cortina dresser that was part of a matching set with the sleigh bed, end tables, and armoire. The whole room oozed old world opulence and was the complete opposite of my tastes, but the interior designer my parents had brought in when they'd bought the house had sold my mother on the idea of keeping to the historic feel of the neighborhood. At eighteen, I'd found myself living in a bedroom designed for an eighty-year-old.

I dug into the drawer and found an old pair of gym shorts. I hastened to undress before Brielle came out of the bathroom. After deciding to leave my white undershirt on, I pulled up the shorts. Seconds later, Brielle poked her head out and I caught a glimpse of her bare shoulder.

"Umm, I don't suppose you have a t-shirt I could borrow? I hadn't planned on sharing a room with you and the only thing I have to sleep in isn't exactly appropriate."

My mind went to a dirty place as I imagined Brielle in lingerie, but I quickly shook the image from my head. "Sure." I went back to the dresser and retrieved an old baseball tee from when I'd played in high school. It was well worn, making it extra soft, which I knew she'd appreciate. Brielle had a thing for soft materials and it always made me laugh when I caught her petting the throw blanket while we watched TV together at home. I handed her the shirt. "Here you go."

"Thanks." The door shut again, but then she opened it a few seconds later. She looked adorable in my giant t-shirt. Her legs were bare and I wondered what she had on underneath my shirt. My cock jerked.

Friends. Just friends.

She pulled back the blanket and got into the queen-sized bed. "I'm stealing this shirt, by the way. It's really soft."

I grinned. "It's yours." It looked better on her anyway. Then I went to the bathroom to wash up and brush my teeth. The room smelled like her peony body cream that I'd become accustomed to and I found it comforting. She was always lathering it on because she said it kept her skin from getting ashy, especially in the cold winter months.

When I returned to the bedroom, I hesitated beside the bed.

Brielle must've noticed. "Yes, I'm sure. Stop being a dork and get in bed." She'd gotten really good at reading my mind since we'd moved in together.

I pulled back the blanket and slid between the sheets, while keeping as close to the edge of the bed as possible. I'd never shared a bed with a woman that I wasn't dating. I didn't do the one-night-stand thing. It was a little weird lying there with my friend and roommate. Her silence told me that she felt it, too. While we'd been closer together on the couch at home many times, there was an intimacy about sharing a bed that made this different.

She reached over and turned out the light on her nightstand, so I did the same. "Good night," she whispered in the dark and I felt her turn onto her side.

"Good night, Elle. Thanks again for coming with me."

"Stop thanking me or I'm going to go home."

I laughed and some of the awkwardness melted away. "Roger that." It took hardly any time at all for me to fall asleep.

FOUR

BRIELLE

Keith's parents house had more people in it than I could count. Between the decorators and the caterers and what I presumed was the house staff, I struggled to figure out how the party guests would all fit once they'd arrived, too. To say that I hadn't been prepared for such a lavish affair would be an understatement. Mrs. Hart had a team of people come to the house to get us women ready like it was a wedding. Keith's mom and Caroline acted like it was totally normal to have full hair and make up artists working on them in the master suite. Heck, it probably was normal for them. While I was used to that to a certain extent as an anchor, I hadn't expected to have the full royal treatment for this party. Admittedly, it made me a bit nervous.

Mrs. Hart was on a headset talking to event planners and caterers and God-knows who else pretty much the entire time. Caroline was writing a speech for the senator she worked for on her tablet, and I couldn't help but notice how tired she looked. I felt for her. I could only imagine that birthing the Hart's first grandchild would be quite the experience.

As for me, I flipped through a magazine trying not to stare

too much at the room we were in. The master suite encompassed half of the top floor. It had its own fireplace and the plushest cream-colored carpet I'd ever walked on. We were set up in the dressing area—I couldn't possibly call it a closet— which was attached to the bathroom. A canvas drop cloth had been laid down so as not to dirty the carpet and there was a long vanity that rivaled those in dressing rooms on set. The built-in cabinetry created the perfect display for all of Mrs. Hart's designer clothes, shoes, and handbags. There was even a display case for her jewelry. While it was all wildly over-the-top, a small part of me was envious. I mean, what girl wouldn't want a closet like that? It even had a crystal chandelier.

It was a bit awkward to not be talking to Caroline and Mrs. Hart, but I was also grateful that they were occupied so I didn't have to force conversation. Once my hair and makeup were done, I went back to Keith's room to get dressed. We'd shared a bed the night before and I'd tried not to make a thing of it. It had certainly been strange, but at the same time it had been kind of nice. It'd been a few months since I'd shared my bed with a man and there was something comforting about having a big, strong body cuddled up beside you. Granted, Keith and I hadn't cuddled. Correction: not on purpose, anyway. When I'd woken up that morning, I'd been pressed up against him with my hand on his chest, but he'd been sound asleep, so I had moved before he could notice.

I unzipped the garment bag that hung on the back of the bathroom door to unveil my slinky new pine-green gown, courtesy of Keith. It was a satin slim-line silhouette with a V-neck and spaghetti straps that crisscrossed in the middle of the low cut open back. When I'd tried it on at the store, I'd felt like a goddess and I was beyond excited to wear it that evening. I untied the robe that Mrs. Hart had loaned me while we were getting ready and dropped it onto the bed, then I relieved my dress of its hanger and slid it up over my hips and onto my shoulders. The satin prevented me from wearing anything underneath, which I suppose was scandalous in a room of some of the most powerful people in America, but it was also a little empowering. Besides, the soft satin felt fantastic against my bare skin.

I slipped my feet into my black stilettos, also new and courtesy of Keith, then retrieved my jewelry from the dresser. After fastening the simple silver drop necklace around my neck, I slipped my diamond studs into my ears. I'd bought them for myself when I made anchor, figuring I deserved a little something special to wear on camera. I made my way into the bathroom and check myself in the full-length mirror behind the door. If I dare say so myself, I looked good. Damn good. I was almost pissed that I had zero chance of getting laid that night because with the way I was looking, it'd be a guarantee had I been on an actual date.

How long had it been? Three months? Four? Too long.

A soft knock rapped on the bedroom door. "Elle, you in there?"

"Come in." I took a deep breath and fluffed the soft curls draped around my shoulders before stepping back into the bedroom. Keith was already in his tuxedo, looking dapper as can be. I'd become accustomed to seeing him jeans and a t-shirt —which he also managed to make look good—but this? This was something else. His normally shaggy, light-brown hair was parted on the side and styled to perfection. It reminded me of Jake Gyllenhaal in *Spiderman.* The black jacket strained against his broad shoulders and chest and rippled over his biceps. *Holy shit, my roommate was hot.* I could practically feel myself panting. All I could think about was grabbing him by that tie and—

"Whoa, Elle. You look unbelievable." His copper eyes darkened as they drifted down my body.

Was he checking me out? I tucked my shoulders back slightly, so that my boobs were on display in their most favorable light. They were easily one of my best assets. "Thank you. You look incredibly handsome."

His jaw hung slack and a wave of satisfaction washed over me. "That dress is...wow." He moved across the room so he was only a mere foot away from me.

I felt my face heat up. "Thanks for buying it for me."

He bit his bottom lip. "I might have to give you my credit card more often."

I laughed. "I'm glad you like."

"I do." His voice dropped to a near whisper. "Almost *too* much."

My breath caught in my chest. I'd seen that look of his before, but it had never been directed at me. Admittedly, a tiny jealousy monster inside me had wanted to slay all of his ex-girlfriends, because that look...

It meant business.

His hand landed on my hip and my heart thumped hard against my ribs. He eyed my mouth like he was starving and I was the only cure for his hunger. I wanted to satisfy that urge—oh, how I wanted to—but we couldn't. We were *friends*. Roommates. Crossing that line would be disastrous.

I cleared my throat and took a step back, breaking whatever trance had hung between us. "Is the party starting?"

He stumbled back a step or two and slid his hands into his pockets. "Yes. A few senators have arrived."

I nodded. "We should go downstairs then."

"Right."

I stepped past him and headed for the door, feeling his presence behind me as I approached the top of the steps and reached for the banister. Once on the first floor, Keith snapped to my side and bent toward my ear. "I'll stick with you all night. We'll be obligated to say hello to everyone, but then we can do our own thing."

I smiled up at him.

One of the hired servers for the evening came by with a tray of champagne and offered some to us, which we gladly took. My nerves were tight, so I welcomed a little relief from the alcohol. Politicians milled about the first floor, chatting animatedly with one another. It reminded me a lot of the parties I'd accompanied Mitchell to and a sourness crept into my gut. I lifted the flute to my lips and took a sip, the bubbles tickling the roof of my mouth. The Hart's had spared no expense. The champagne was undoubtedly high-end.

As we made our way through the house, I noticed all the furniture had been replaced by several small tables, and the holiday decorations had quadrupled since the day before. It looked like the Macy's in Herald Square had thrown up in the living room. Sure, it was lovely. Very festive. But it was a bit over-the-top.

Keith offered me his arm, which I took, as we milled through the crowd of men in tuxedos and women in evening gowns. I was grateful that I hadn't argued with Keith about buying me a dress. I would've stuck out like a sore thumb had I worn one of the cocktail dresses I had in my closet. Keith bowed his head at several of the guests, but he hadn't bothered to stop and chat. Fine by me.

We found Corbett and Caroline in the dining room, which had been cleared of the large oak table that had sat in the middle of it the day before. Multiple high-top bar tables filled the room instead. I was glad to see familiar faces, even if they weren't exactly friendly.

"Caroline, you look lovely," I said as we greeted them. Her

navy, empire-waisted dress sufficiently hid her baby bump, but it flattered her as well. She had ivory skin and the dark-blue complimented her fair tone. Her mousy brown hair was pulled back into a chignon, which reminded me of Mrs. Hart's the day before. Caroline's sharp pointy nose and diamond-shaped face, were highlighted by her tightly pulled hair. I wouldn't call her a beautiful woman, but she was pretty. There was something intimidating in her muddy brown eyes, though. She looked like she belonged in politics.

"Thank you." She offered me a small smile. "You look delightful yourself."

Before I could respond, the music that played through the built-in speakers changed dramatically from a soft piano concerto to an up-tempo jazz song that was heavy on the saxophone. It was jarring enough to catch everyone's attention. Just in time to see Keith's parents descend the stairs.

I giggled to myself. *Well played, Lemon Hart.*

While I had joked the night before about Keith being adopted, there was no way I'd believe it. He looked an awful lot like his father. Senator Hart was a man of large stature. Like Keith, he was tall, and he was built big. Not fat, but thick. Keith wore it well with his ample muscles, and I imagined that the senator had had a similar body type when he was younger and in the army. His copper eyes were identical to Keith's and he had the same strong features. The main difference was his crew cut. Keith's hair was on the longer side and, having met his father, I wondered if he'd chosen that style on purpose.

Lemon Hart was a vision in her gold, jacquard, off-the-shoulder, tiered mermaid gown. Undoubtedly, it'd been custom made for her. Her ash brown hair was pulled back into a chignon, much like the one Caroline sported, and her makeup was just enough for the formal occasion without being overdone.

While the guests fussed over the hosts, Keith asked Caroline, "Did you have a chance to speak with Senator Jansen?"

She nodded. "Yes. I made him aware of our situation. Last night, your mother graciously offered to help take care of the baby so that I won't have to take more than a month off of work."

A sadness struck my chest. I understood being ambitious. And, as a woman of color, I knew that I'd have to go above and beyond to keep from being usurped in my career, as awful as that reality was. That being said, when I had kids, I'd want to be there as much as possible. My career would have to wait. I guess politics was different, though. Undoubtedly, it wasn't easy being a woman on Capital Hill. The night before, Caroline had hinted that she aspired to run for office one day. Taking time off to raise a child would put her behind, so I understood that, but it still made me sad. Why couldn't women have both?

"That's very nice." Keith sounded happy for her, but I saw right through it. I wouldn't take kindly to Lemon Hart being around to raise my kid every day, either. I felt for Caroline, and for Keith's future wife. Although, I had a feeling that Keith would do a much better job of insulating his new family from his parents than Corbett was.

A frenzied woman in a headset wearing black pants and a black button-down collared shirt approached us. "It's time for the family portraits. Senator Hart would like them taken by the tree and the fireplace in the sitting room."

Keith grabbed my hand and I followed him into the room where we'd had cocktails the night before. Keith's parents were already there, along with a photographer. A Christmas tree that hadn't been there the day before was perched beside the fireplace. It was adorned with white lights as well as red and gold ornaments.

Senator Hart waved the family over. "Gather around. Let's get this finished so we can enjoy the party."

"Soirée," Mrs. Hart corrected.

Keith released my hand, handed me his champagne, and took his place beside his mother, while Corbett filed in next to his father. Caroline stepped in beside her husband. I hung around by the photographer.

"Brielle, please join us," Senator Hart said.

"That's very kind of you, Senator, but I understand that it's a family photo."

"Nonsense." He waved me over. "Stand next to Keith." He wasn't asking.

I placed our champagne flutes down on one of the bistro tables and took the spot beside Keith. My friend and *pretend* boyfriend, Keith. The photographer snapped several photos before telling us he'd gotten what he'd needed.

"Fabulous," Mrs. Hart said. "Have you taken shots of the children?"

"I got some of those two," he pointed to Corbett and Caroline, "but not of the other two."

Mrs. Hart shooed Keith and I toward the center of the fireplace.

Keith stood beside me and in my heels, I was only about four inches shorter than him. He put his arm behind my back. In comparison to the heat emanating off of the fireplace, his hand felt cold when it settled onto my bare back, sending a shiver up my spine. His hand was large enough to stretch nearly across my entire lower back. I followed suit and wrapped my arm behind his waist.

The photographer took a few photos, then shook his head. "Too stiff. Make like you love each other."

My body tensed and I felt my face flush. Keith didn't move right away, but eventually he took charge and pushed me forward a few steps so that he was behind me. His arms draped over mine and his hands clasped around my mid-section. It took a few seconds for me to figure out what to do with my hands, but I ended up settling them onto his forearms. He pressed up against my back and I could feel the bulge in his pants pressed against my backside. While he didn't feel hard, it was obvious that he was well-endowed in the penis department. The apex between my thighs tingled.

Being that close to him felt good. Too good. He made me feel safe and protected. Plus, he smelled incredible. His cologne was warm and spicy, which was quite fitting for winter. I wanted to stay wrapped up in his arms all night.

The photographer had other plans. "All set. Thank you."

Keith didn't release me right away and I wondered if perhaps he was feeling it, too. Except going there would ruin everything, and we couldn't do that. I patted his arms and he let go, then I stepped forward and retrieved my champagne from the table where I'd left it, without looking back at him.

His arm brushed mine as he reached for his champagne. When I glanced up at him, he gave me one of his seal-the-deal smiles. *There are the tingles again.*

I brought the flute to my lips.

Senator Hart placed a hand on Keith's shoulder. "Come you two. There are some people I'd like you to meet."

We spent the next two hours chatting with enough senators that I'd lost count. Most of them were nice, but they all had the same holier-than-thou attitude. Although, I did get to meet Senator Armstrong from New York and *he* had recognized *me.* I had a moment then. He'd told me he often watched my show, then he'd asked to take a photo with me, which I happily obliged. That one was going in my portfolio. Senator Hart had seen the whole exchange and I hoped it helped Keith impress his father.

When we'd finally gotten a break from networking, Keith and I snuck out onto the patio behind the house, which had been tented and heated for the occasion. Thankfully, the few people who were out there, seemed disinterested in chatting with us. The tent was lit with twinkling lights and instrumental holiday music played over the speakers. We found an empty table and sat down for the first time all evening. My feet were grateful to get a break from the four-inch stilettos I'd been balancing on all evening.

"This is exhausting. I can't believe you have to do this every year."

He chuckled. "I've gotten used to it, but it's still not my scene. Despite what my parents think, I'll never go into politics."

I grinned. "Good. I don't know how many of these things I could tolerate going to as your fake-girlfriend."

The corners of his mouth dipped slightly. "I really appreciate you doing this. I know it's a lot, but the thought alone of having to endure tonight with Megan makes me cringe. Thanks for talking me out of that one."

"Of course. Make sure you remember that I was right and you were wrong next time you try to argue with me."

"Yeah, yeah." He loosened his tie a tiny bit. "Despite everything, I'm having a great time with you. Somehow, you've managed to make this a fun trip."

That made me smile. "It really has been. Last night was great. It was cool to see Georgetown and the light art exhibit." I shrugged. "Even this party isn't all that bad. It isn't often I'm able to get all dolled up. It's nice every now and again."

His copper eyes gleamed. "From now on, when were both home on a Friday, we're having formal night. I'll put on a suit and you can wear," his gaze dipped to my dress, "that."

I laughed. "That's ridiculous."

He shook his head. "Not at all. You belong in that dress."

My face warmed at his flattery. I changed the subject. "Hey, so how cool is it that Senator Armstrong watches me on TV?"

"Way cool." He winked.

"Don't make fun."

"All right, yeah, it's fucking awesome."

I shook my head and breathed out a laugh.

"There you are," an unmistakable woman's voice with a formal southern accent called from behind me. "There is someone I would like you to meet."

Keith sighed and stood, turning it on in a flash. That was one ability he'd inherited from his parents. He could snap into that role in an instant.

I stood as well and straightened out my dress before turning to face Mrs. Hart and whoever it was we had to meet.

"Millicent Lumley, this is my son Keith and his girlfriend, Brielle Jackson."

Keith and I both shook the woman's hand. She looked as though she were in her mid-forties and she had enviable dark red hair.

"Millicent is a producer for the morning show on USBC here in Washington. Brielle is an anchor for your network in New York."

Well, I certainly hadn't expected that. I tried to swallow my shock.

Millicent's drawn on brows arched up. "Is that so? Which show do you anchor?"

"The News at Noon. I'm also a general reporter for the morning show."

Millicent nodded approvingly. "That's quite an accomplishment for someone so young. If you don't mind me asking, how old are you?"

I straightened my back. "I'm twenty-four, but I was twenty-three when I started as an anchor."

She let out a hum.

I explained how I'd won an AP Award, which had garnered me attention from the network executives.

"Congratulations. Keep that up and you'll have a very successful career." She reached into her clutch and fished out a business card. "If you ever consider relocating to D.C., give me a call."

I took the card. "Thank you, Ms. Lumley. I'll keep that in mind."

"Please do. I must be going now, but it was a pleasure to meet you both."

"Likewise," I said.

She turned to Mrs. Hart. "Another wonderful event, Lemon. Thank you for inviting me."

"Of course. I am delighted you could make it." Mrs. Hart grabbed Millicent's hands and they gave each other air kisses by each cheek, then Millicent left.

Mrs. Hart placed her hand on my bicep. "Millicent is a dear friend. I am elated that you got to meet her. When you and Keith move to Washington, she will certainly find you a spot on her show."

I choked on my saliva.

"Mother," Keith snapped. "Enough."

She put her hands up and her smug expression said, *I've don't nothing wrong.*

Keith continued, "I'm not moving to D.C."

"Do not be silly, Keith. When your father becomes president, you will be obligated to be here with your family." She turned to me with a sickeningly sweet grin and said, "Brielle would have her pick of networks in Washington, then. I bet you could even have your own show, sugar."

My eyes widened. I knew what she was up to. I had to give it to her though, Lemon Hart was a skilled manipulator. Unfortunately for her, I wasn't easily assuaged.

"That's a nice idea, Mrs. Hart, but I'm determined to make it in my career on my own. I would never use your husband's connections to get me there. Just like I don't use my parents' careers to further my own."

Her hand covered her chest. "Bless your heart. How noble of you, sugar. Do not discount it, though. Once you marry my son, you will be a part of the first family one day and there will be no hiding that fact."

Keith stepped between us. "Mother, stop harassing my girlfriend into agreeing to your agenda. And knock it off with this marriage business. Brielle and I are dating. Don't push it."

She waved him off. "Darling, please. You are making a scene out of nothing. I am simply helping Brielle make important connections. That is all."

"Lemon?" Senator Hart appeared at the patio door. "It is time to make our important announcement."

"Yes of course. Come along now," she ordered in a tone that said we had no option but to follow her.

I sighed. While I knew that my reprieve came at the expense of Caroline, I was grateful that I was no longer the center of Lemon Hart's attention. She was a frightening woman, to say the least. I moved forward to follow, but Keith grabbed my hand and held me back.

He bent to my ear and whispered, "I'm sorry. I knew she'd try to ambush you at some point, but I hadn't expected her to be that insistent."

Was I unhappy with his mother for the way she'd addressed me? Absolutely, but I was more pissed off about how she thought she could dictate the terms of her son's life. "I'm fine, Keith." I tenderly placed my hand on his forearm. "I'm sorry you have to put up with that. I can't imagine what they've put you through all these years."

He gave me a lopsided grin and held his hand out for me to take, which I did. "Come on, we'd better go watch them throw Corbett and Caroline to the wolves."

Once inside, we made our way to the staircase overlooking the foyer. It opened up to the dining room on one side and the formal living room on the other, and we stood at the bottom of it. Senator and Mrs. Hart were already perched halfway up with Corbett and Caroline just below them. The guests filed around.

"Good evening. Lemon and I are overjoyed that you could all join us this evening for our annual holiday soirée."

Everyone clapped at Senator Hart's welcome.

"Our family has some wonderful news that we would like to share with all of you. Many of you know my son, Corbett. He is my Legislative Director. And his wife, our darling daughter-in-law, Caroline, who is the Assistant Press Secretary for Senator Jansen." He found the other senator in the crowd and gave him a nod before continuing. "We are pleased to announce that Corbett and Caroline are expecting their first child in May."

The crowd applauded and shouted their congratulations. I had to give it to Caroline. Smiled and took it like a pro. Perhaps she fit into this family better than I'd thought. Corbett wrapped an arm around his wife and kissed her.

Mrs. Hart raised her hand silencing the crowd. "Thank you for your well wishes and enthusiasm. Certainly, we are delighted with this news. I would also like to acknowledge another member of our family." She looked straight at Keith and me. "Keith, Brielle, come on up here."

Keith's hand tightened around mine as we ascended a few steps up toward them.

His mother continued, "Our son Keith is joining us from New York this weekend along with his long-time, serious girl-friend, Brielle Jackson, whom we simply adore. You may recognize Brielle. She is an award-winning journalist and is the youngest anchor for USBC in New York. We are rather proud of her and are delighted that she was able to join us this year. Are they not adorable?"

The crowd awed and laughed.

My face felt like it was on fire. Granted, I was no stranger to being the center of attention, but I didn't care for being put on the spot. And I most definitely didn't take kindly to Mrs. Hart's attempt to use me to impress, but I had more class than she did, so I would play along for her friends. I wouldn't let her behavior slide though. Judging by the tick in Keith's jaw, I didn't suspect he would either.

And then she made it worse. "Give us a kiss you two."

My eyes widened.

Keith protested, "Mother, these people don't want to see that."

Someone from the crowd, who had clearly been overserved judging by his slurring, starting chanting, "Kiss her" like we were the bride and groom at a wedding. Others joined in.

Keith looked down at me, sweat beaded above his brow, and his eyes pleaded for help.

I gave him an almost imperceptible nod, telling him that it was all right.

He bent his face toward me and I took a deep breath in as his lips quickly grazed against mine before pulling away. No harm done.

Mrs. Hart responded by saying, "Goodness, Keith, I hope you are more romantic than that."

Another drunk someone shouted, "Give her a real kiss."

The awkward tension in the room was palpable and the

longer we prolonged it, the worse it became. His copper eyes stared into mine as if to say, *I'm sorry, but I think we have to do this.*

I saved him the agony. My heart hammered in my chest as I wrapped my arms behind his neck and pulled him to me. His hands snaked around to my back as his lips met mine. This was no soft peck like the last time. My eyes fluttered shut as his lower lip slid directly into my mouth and I tasted the peppery red wine he'd been drinking. With great care, his lips moved around mine and the hammering in my chest subsided. He was gentle, which was a bit of a mind-fuck because I'd never think to use the word gentle to describe Keith.

His fingers dug into my back, tugging my body toward him, and I leaned into his hard chest. Without a doubt, something about that kiss felt right and tingles spread throughout my body. I'd nearly forgotten that we were in a room full of some of the most powerful people in America.

Until I heard the applause. I wasn't sure if it had been happening the whole time Keith had been kissing me or if it had just started, but either way it startled me. I released his lip and slowly backed my head away, taking a second before opening my eyes because once I did, it would be real, and I knew nothing would ever be the same.

FIVE

KEITH

I'd kissed Brielle. My Elle. *Fuck.*

Still holding her close, I opened my eyelids a second before she did. Her pupils were large and her fiery gaze told me she'd felt it, too. That was no ordinary kiss. *Actors do this all of the time*, I'd told myself before I'd gone for it. But there was no way in hell I'd believe that fake kisses felt like that. Shit, I'd had real kisses that hadn't felt like that. It was good. Too good. Her warm mouth was a sanctuary that had managed to dispel all of my nervousness. When she'd pulled away, I had nearly cried out to protest the loss, but the sounds of the crowd surrounding us had snapped me to reality.

Her lips were still parted and they were slick with the evidence of our kiss. I was tempted to claim her mouth again, but before I could make my move, Corbett's hand landed on my shoulder, destroying the moment. I released Brielle and turned up toward my brother.

"Bedroom is upstairs."

In my stupor, I failed to think of a comeback. Before I could stop her, Brielle descended the steps and I followed. She didn't wait for me as she weaved through the crowd. Several of the guests stopped me to talk, and with each sentence, Brielle got further away. Eventually, I lost sight of her entirely and that caused my chest to ache.

It took nearly twenty minutes before I could extricate myself from the Tennessee senators. By then, I had no idea where she'd gone. I searched both living rooms and the patio out back, coming up empty. I made my way to the dining room and caught a glimpse of her over in a corner speaking with Senator Patten from New Jersey. I dodged a few more attempts to gain my attention and came up beside her.

She didn't stop her conversation to acknowledge me. "Social media is one of the biggest hurdles our nation is facing when it comes to stopping these gangs from thriving. It gives them an audience they wouldn't otherwise have and is opening up new channels for recruitment while also giving them a plethora of information about people that can be used to force their will onto others."

Senator Patten nodded. "I see your point."

"Let's look at an example from your state. Take MS-13 in Newark. About six weeks ago a fourteen-year-old boy, Luis Santiago, was jumped in because he lived in their territory. The gang threatened to hurt his parents and his little sister if he didn't join them and they used information they'd learned from his Facebook to prove to him that they could easily harm his loved ones."

She was animated as she spoke and I could feel the energy flowing from her. Gang violence was something Brielle had been passionate about for as long as I'd known her. A friend she'd had growing up had gotten into gang life and ended up in prison with a thirty-year sentence. According to her, he'd been a good kid and had a lot going for him. His life could've been spared if only he hadn't been tempted into the gang.

As a journalist, Brielle made it her mission to do something to fix America's gang problem. That's how she wound up winning that AP Award. She waltzed right into a crew of Bloods and gained their trust. After several months, she'd gotten them to interview with her on camera and open up about why they'd chosen gang life. It was brilliant.

She continued, "As is the gang's ritual for the jumping in ceremony, three fully grown men pummeled Luis for thirteen seconds. They nearly killed him. He'll be on dialysis for the rest of his life unless he gets a new kidney now."

The senator looked appalled. "I'm sorry to admit that I haven't heard this."

"Happens every day. Luis Santiago was at the top of his class and dreamed of becoming a pilot in the Airforce. He had a promising future ahead of him." She shook her head. "But now that he's jumped in, he's MS-13 for life and they'll never let him go. All because this *child* had to protect his family."

Senator Patten sighed and his eyes dimmed. He reached into his jacket and pulled a business card from the inside pocket. "I'd like to talk to you more about this. Perhaps we can discuss a way we can work together going forward." He handed her his card.

"Absolutely, Senator. Thank you."

The short, stubby man turned toward me. "You've got a good one here, Mr. Hart. Don't let her go."

I grinned and looked straight at Brielle. "I won't."

The senator excused himself, leaving me with Brielle. "Seems you made quite an impression on Senator Patten."

She sighed. "I hope so. The Newark clique of MS-13 is small in comparison to some other gangs in the area, but they're the deadliest. Now is the time to get ahead of it before they get too large."

I smiled at her.

"What?"

"It's sexy when you get all worked up like this. Your intelligence and your compassion are showing."

She shifted on her feet.

Strike number two. *Dang, Keith can't you do anything right?* I hadn't meant to call her sexy, even though I thought it. We'd joked around with each other like that plenty of times before, but this time it felt different. I'd kissed her and just like that our friendship had changed.

I ran my hand over my chin. "Elle, we should talk."

She nodded. "Not now." She went to put her hand on my arm, like she'd done so many times before, but stopped herself. "I'm going to grab a drink." She took a few steps away from me, then turned and added. "Why don't you mingle here for a little bit. I'll catch up with you later."

She was gone before I could stop her.

IT WAS APPROACHING midnight by the time the party wound down. It'd been a couple of hours since I'd even seen Brielle. The crowd had thinned considerably, so I decided to do a lap in search of her, but I came up empty. I found Caroline seated in a chair at one of the small tables in the living room. She looked overdue for bed.

"Hey. You feeling okay?"

She nodded. "Just tired. This baby seems to suck all of my energy."

I glanced around for my brother. "Where's Corbett?"

"He's saying goodbye. We're heading home soon."

I nodded. "Good. You can always go rest in one of the guest rooms."

"I'll be fine."

I was about to walk away, but decided to ask, "Have you seen Brielle?"

She pointed toward the stairs. "She went up about fifteen minutes ago."

I thanked her and gave her a hug goodbye.

My hand was already on the banister, when I had an idea. I went to the kitchen instead and asked the staff for two mugs of chamomile tea. Once I had those in hand, I headed to my room. The door was closed, so I cradled both mugs in one hand and knocked. "Elle? It's me. Can I come in?" I held my breath.

"Sure."

I twisted the knob and entered my bedroom. Brielle was standing there in my t-shirt and it rode up her bare legs as she reached for the hanger to hook her dress on. My gaze fell to her ass, which was fucking perfect, and I willed the shirt to lift just a little higher so I could see what she had on underneath.

And then I came to my senses.

"I brought you some tea." I placed it down on her nightstand.

"Thanks." She zipped up her garment bag, tucking the dress neatly inside. Then she made a wide circle around me to get into bed. She'd already washed her makeup off and she was just as beautiful without it. More-so even. She grabbed the mug and took a sip while propped up against the headboard. "This is perfect. I'm exhausted."

"Yeah, I know these things can be a lot. I'm pretty tired, too." I put my mug down on the dresser so I could remove my jacket.

"It was good, though. I met some really interesting people."

"I'm glad." I loosened my tie and pulled the tail through the knot to undo it.

"I spoke to several senators about the gang violence in their states. I think I gave them a lot to think about. At least I hope I did." She sipped her tea.

"That's great." I undid the cufflinks and placed them on the dresser beside my tie.

"Yeah."

I knew we had to discuss that kiss, but I wasn't sure how to bring it up and she didn't seem like she was eager to discuss it either. I'd removed as many layers as was appropriate in front of her, so I had to make my way into the bathroom to fully change. After brushing my teeth, I went back into the bedroom to find her laying down with her eyes closed.

Looked like we wouldn't be discussing it at all that night.

SOMETHING TICKLED MY NECK, causing me to wake. Sunlight streamed into the room and it took me a few seconds to remember where I was. The tickling sensation had come from the hair of the woman who was cuddled up against me. In my sleepy haze, I assumed it was Megan. I closed my eyes again because I could've easily gone back to sleep, but not a minute later, my eyes sprang open as I remembered I had broken up with Megan and I was sharing a bed with Brielle—my *friend*.

She had her head on my shoulder and her hand was resting on my chest. The low whisper of her breathing told me she was sound asleep. My immediate inclination was to slide out from underneath her and get up, but I liked the weight of her on me. The sweet smell of peonies tantalized my nostrils and the warmth of her body was soothing. I thought perhaps we could lay there like that for a little while as long as I pretended to be asleep. And then the memory of our kiss came flooding back to me.

For the first time in our entire friendship, things had been awkward between us. One thing I treasured about my relationship with Brielle was how effortless it was, but it was clear that something had changed. That kiss had shifted something between us. If I was being honest, I wanted to kiss her again. As cliché as it sounds, if kissing her was truly wrong, then why had it felt so right?

I thought about the friendship we'd fostered over the years. Brielle was someone I knew I'd always have in my corner no matter what. If I needed her, she'd be there, and vice versa. People as real and as genuine as Brielle didn't come along very often. We'd never dated because the timing had never been right and then we'd passed the point of that being a possibility. Our friendship was solid and trying to go down the road of dating would surely ruin that. If things didn't work out, I'd never forgive myself for losing one of my best friends.

I'd really fucked things up. I never should have kissed her like that. Could I have kept it tamer? Sure, but once her lips had been entangled with mine, I'd no longer been in control. My body had taken over and I'd given into the pleasure. That had been wrong of me. And I could only pray she'd forgive me, so we could move forward like it had never happened.

Although, something told me that'd be much easier said than done. I was unlikely to forget how incredible she felt anytime soon—if ever.

As badly as I wanted to stay in bed with her, it wasn't right. I shimmied myself out from beneath her, letting her head ease onto my pillow and her hand drift down to the mattress. Once my feet were on the ground and I noticed she was still asleep, I sighed with relief. She'd never have to know we were cuddling. After grabbing my phone off the night stand, I checked the time finding that it was just after nine a.m. Church started at ten-thirty, and while I never went on my own, being with my parents made my attendance non-negotiable. I crept around the bed and went into the bathroom to shower.

Afterwards, I realized I'd forgotten to grab clothes to change into, so I wrapped the towel around my waist and quietly opened the door to the bedroom. I found Brielle lying in bed awake. Being that we were roommates, she'd seen me in a towel before, hell, she'd even seen me in my underwear, but things were different then. *Fuck.*

"Good morning," I said as I hastened to the dresser, grabbing the first thing my hand landed on in the drawer.

"Morning," she grumbled in her sleepy voice. When she noticed me standing there in the towel, she darted her eyes away.

"Forgot to grab my clothes. Sorry." I went to the armoire for a shirt.

"It's fine." She stared down at the sheets.

With clothes in hand, I scurried back into the bathroom and shut the door, breathing out in relief. I rubbed a hand over my freshly shaved face. I'd give anything to go back to the night before so I could take back that kiss.

I fastened the buttons on my white, long-sleeved button-down before tucking it into the waistband of my navy slacks. Perhaps the best thing to do would be to pretend like it had never happened. Then, we could just go back to normal.

After combing my hair, parting it on the side, I added some pomade and took a good look at myself in the mirror. My father's eyes stared back at me. If he seriously made a bid for the White House, I'd be spending a lot more time looking at myself in that particular mirror. Despite my parents' insistence, I'd never move to D.C. because New York was my home, but I would be the dutiful son and attend what was absolutely required of me. For all my parent's flaws, I'd love to see my father's presidential dreams come true for him.

That being said, I needed to have a conversation with Mother because the way she'd used Brielle the night before was unacceptable. I should probably apologize to Brielle for that, too. I opened the door and went back to the bedroom.

Brielle was standing beside the bed packing her bag while wearing black palazzo pants and a silver long-sleeved body suit. The tight-fitting top showed off her narrow waist and her full, perky tits. I really needed to get control of myself. Checking out Brielle was not how I'd get us back to normal.

She glanced at me. "You look dapper."

"Uh, thanks. I've got to go to church with the family at ten-thirty. You don't have to come, unless you want to."

She cocked her head to the side. "You're going to church?"

I huffed. "Yeah. Not really negotiable when I'm home. My parents are Southern Baptists through and through."

"Do you want me to go?"

Yes, of course. "Only if you want to. Not going to force that on you. You've done more than enough for me this weekend."

She stiffened.

I swallowed. "Look, Elle, I'm really sorry."

She put up a hand. "No need to apologize. I knew what I'd signed up for when I'd agreed to come here as your pretend girlfriend. Let's not make a thing of it."

While I should've been relieved by her words, I wasn't. I don't know what I'd expected to happen, but a big part of me wanted her to say that she had felt it, too. "Right. Of course. Well, thanks."

She nodded. "I'll go to church with you, but if your mother pulls another stunt like last night where she thinks she can parade me around like I hadn't just met her less than forty-eight hours ago, I might not be so nice."

I retrieved a tie from the armoire and placed it around my neck. "Totally understandable. And don't worry, I'm going to have a talk with her about that." I looped my tie around itself to form a knot. "I can't promise it'll do much, because Mother has always been about what's best for Lemon Hart, spare no expense—including others' feelings, but she crossed a line last night. I won't let her get off that easily."

She took a seat on the bed to put on her shoes and sighed. "You don't have to make waves on my account. Your mother isn't the first political type I've had to deal with. And while I would love to put her in her place, if it isn't going to do any good, then let's just let it go. No point in ruffling feathers if she won't learn the lesson." She tugged the zippers up on the inside of her short boots. "Last night, I was ready to tear into her, but now that I've slept on it, she isn't worth it. None of it will matter once we leave here and return to reality anyway."

Yet another reason why I adored Brielle. She was constantly looking out for me, no matter what. I'd never had someone in my corner like that before. I added that to the list of why we couldn't jeopardize our friendship. I gave her a lopsided grin. "You're one of the best friends I've got, you know that?"

She stood and stepped up to me, getting close enough to make me question her plan, and my body immediately froze, excited by the prospect of perhaps getting another kiss. So much for my will-power. Clearly, Brielle was less affected than I had been because all she did was reach for the knot on my tie to straighten it.

"You're one of my best friends, too." She smiled as she folded my collar down.

Maybe we'd be able to get back to normal after all. That thought made me sadder than it should have.

SIX

BRIELLE

We'd been back from D.C. for four days and I still couldn't shake that kiss. That being said, I was trying my damndest to pretend like nothing had happened between us. Truth? Playing the role of Keith's girlfriend was more fun than I'd like to admit. Dealing with his family, not so much, but having him on my arm, sharing his bed, kissing him...

I turned the knob to our apartment. I'd been at the studio for longer than usual and I was looking forward to a hot bath, a glass of wine, and an early night. When I got into our apartment, I stopped in my tracks. Keith was in the kitchen stirring a pot on the stove. Keith didn't cook. If it didn't come frozen or from a restaurant, Keith didn't eat. His West Side Wolverines firehouse t-shirt stretched over his biceps and his gray sweats hung low on his hips, showing off his tight backside.

"Hey, Elle," he hollered over his shoulder.

I kicked off my boots and crossed to the kitchen. "Umm, what are you doing?"

"Making us dinner," he replied, casually, as though this was a normal occurrence.

I slid onto one of the stools at the island. The kitchen was a disaster. Eggshells were strewn about the counter and there was so much flour—on everything— it looked like the snow outside had moved indoors. "What are you making?" I asked, afraid of the answer.

"Chicken parm. Got the recipe from one of the guys at work last night and thought I'd try it. His wife is Italian and she's a phenomenal cook. He said this was her grandmother's recipe. Real authentic."

The sauce he was stirring splattered everywhere. The burner was on way too high. I got off my stool and went to the stove to turn the knob and lower the flame. "Too hot and you'll burn the bottom."

"Uh, right. Thanks." He was covered in flour; it was in his tousled hair, down the front of his clothes, and the oak floors looked like they were trying to masquerade as birch.

"While I applaud your efforts, Keith, want to tell me what sparked this?"

He shrugged. "Felt like it. When you texted that you were going to be home late, I thought it'd be a nice surprise." He was up to something.

"Right," I said cautiously. "And the flour? Did you coat the chicken on the floor?"

He actually blushed. A rare look for Keith. "I may have had a little trouble getting the bag open. But don't worry, I'll clean it."

"The bag? You know we have a canister of it right here?" I pointed to the large ceramic container on the counter with a big F on the front that lived next to the sugar. The same sugar he used for his coffee every morning.

"Oh."

I stifled a laugh. "I'm, uh, going to go change out of my work clothes. Then, I'll come help."

"No help needed. I've got this under control. You go relax and I'll let you know when it's ready."

I tiptoed out of the kitchen in an attempt to minimize how much flour I tracked through the house, and went to my bedroom. When I closed the door, I allowed myself to laugh. "Keith Hart, what on earth are you up to?" I whispered.

I stripped out of my work clothes and decided to forego the bath and take a shower instead; that'd be quicker and I was fairly certain Keith was going to need rescuing in the kitchen. He was a notoriously bad cook and having met his family and catching a glimpse of how he'd grown up, I understood why. He'd never had to learn.

Sunday with his family had been fine. We'd gone to church and then had returned to the house for brunch. By the time we'd gotten back, the whole house had been returned to its pre-party state. I had to give it to the staff, they were good. His parents were fine and had even invited me to come to their house in Kentucky for Christmas. I'd lied and said I had plans with my family. Truth was, my mom and dad were spending Christmas in London so I was on my own, but that seemed better than suffering through another few days with Senator and Mrs. Hart. The fact that Keith came from them was still boggling my mind.

After my shower, I put on yoga pants and a Cornell University hoodie, my alma mater, then I rejoined Keith in the kitchen. He was bent over with his head and shoulders in the oven.

"Are you trying to mimic Sylvia Plath?" I asked

"What?"

"The poet."

He pulled out the pan of chicken and set it on the counter. "I know who she is, but what do you mean mimic her?"

"She committed suicide by putting her head in the oven."

"Oh, yeah. No, I'm not trying to off myself. I think there's something wrong with the oven. It's not getting hot."

I went over to check it. Sure enough, it was warm at best. "You're certain you turned it on?"

"Yeah. I hit the power button."

I checked the controls. It was set to one-hundred-seventy degrees. I pressed my lips together to keep from laughing. "Umm, Keith, you didn't set the temperature."

His thick brows furrowed. "What do you mean? I turned it on."

"Yes, but then you have to set how hot you want the oven to be."

"There are different temperatures?"

I nodded and covered my mouth with my fist, trying not to laugh.

"The oven at the firehouse automatically gets hot when it's turned on. I didn't know I had to do something other than hit the button."

I pushed the up arrow to three-hundred-fifty degrees, then grabbed the barely warm pan of chicken and placed it into the oven. "Not to worry, we can salvage this."

He looked defeated.

"Hey, it's all good. It'll be done in about thirty minutes."

He pouted and the urge to suck that lip into my mouth boiled up within me. I wouldn't give into it, though. Keith was one of my very best friends and I couldn't risk losing him. Even though that kiss had been incredible, I wouldn't let myself go there again. No, it was best to pretend like the whole thing had never happened and move on. In fact, I was doing just that. I had a date the next night. I was supposed to have gone the weekend before, but I'd rescheduled when I'd found out about the D.C. trip.

I went to the closet and grabbed a broom and the Swiffer, then went to work cleaning up the mess.

"I said I'd clean. Leave it."

"It's fine. I don't mind."

"Not the point, Elle. I wanted to do something nice for you and here you are cooking for me and cleaning up my mess."

I leaned the broom against the counter. "I appreciate your effort, and this is very nice, but I truly don't mind helping." Besides, cleaning occupied me so that I wasn't thinking about kissing my roommate.

He sighed and began cleaning off the counters. We worked in silence, bit by bit, erasing the evidence of Keith's attempt at dinner. Once it was all back to normal, Keith said, "I'm just going to put on a new shirt."

I nodded. "Good idea."

He came back out a minute later without a shirt on. His six pack abs on full display in all their glory. I salivated.

"Do you think I need to put something on this?" He pointed to a red blotch on his lower abdomen.

I got closer and bent down to take a look. "What'd you do?"

He shrugged. "Hot oil may have splattered up when I was pan frying the chicken."

Without thinking I reached out and touched the spot. His skin was warm and his muscle was solid as a rock. I wanted to lick it. *Wait, no. No, I did not. Keith was my friend. Friend. Friend. Friend.*

"Well? What do you think?"

"It can't hurt to put some antibacterial ointment on it. I have some in the cabinet above my bathroom sink if you need it."

"Okay, thanks."

My eyes followed him as he went toward my room and I squeezed my thighs together.

The oven timer buzzed, so I grabbed the mitts and pulled the chicken out. I wasn't sure how Keith had planned to plate it, so I left it on the counter and poured myself a glass of chardonnay while I waited for him.

When he returned, I told him that the chicken was done and he shooed me from the kitchen so he could serve it. I took a seat at the dining table and he joined me a couple of minutes later, with two plates in hand. Truly touched by his gesture, I swooned a little when he placed the plate of pasta and chicken in front of me. "Thank you."

"Happy to do it." He poured himself some wine and sat down in the seat across from me. "Bon appetit."

I picked up my utensils and cut into the chicken. It was cooked, so we were already off to a good start. Keith watched me intently while I brought the forkful to my mouth and chewed. Once I swallowed, I said, "This is actually pretty good."

"Yeah?" He cut a piece for himself and his brows shot up.

I went for a bite of the spaghetti and immediately regretted it. It crunched in my mouth. I thought about lying to him, but he'd figure it out when he tried to eat it himself. "The pasta is a bit al dente."

He tried his and scrunched up his face. "Fuck. I'm sorry."

I went for another bite of chicken. "Not a big deal. This chicken makes up for it."

He smiled.

"So are you going to tell me what I did to deserve this?"

"I told you I just wanted to do something nice for you."

"Yes, but why?"

He shrugged. "Because. Do I need a reason?"

We hadn't spoken about the weekend in D.C. since we'd left, not even in the car ride on the way home, but I had no doubts that this meal had something to do with that. A piece of me wished Keith felt what I had felt during that kiss, but I knew better than to believe that. I was not his type. Although I often wondered if he even knew what his type was. After meeting his parents, I realized why he had such horrible taste in women. He was always trying to pick women that would please his family. No wonder his relationships never worked out.

Keith took a sip of his wine and a little dribbled down his chin, but he caught it with his napkin. He seemed nervous.

"What's up?" I asked.

"Nothing."

"You're never this quiet."

He shrugged. "Guess I'm a little tired. We didn't get much sleep at work last night."

I wasn't sure if I should believe that excuse or not.

He blinked a few times. "Are you busy tomorrow night? I thought maybe you and I could do something."

I rubbed my lips together. "I can't, sorry. I have a date."

"Oh. Okay, cool."

We continued to eat. Then he broke the silence. "So who's the lucky guy?"

"His name is Paul. He works in the newsroom at USBC."

He nodded. "Cool, cool." He took another sip of his wine. "Where you going?"

"Varsity on Columbus Ave. Apparently it's one of the best places to watch the hockey game."

He narrowed his eyes. "But you don't like hockey."

I shrugged. "I don't mind it. Paul's into it, so why not?"

"Paul. Yeah, sure."

The awkward tension was building between us so I changed the subject. "I spoke with Senator Patten today. That's why I was stuck at work late. He wants to work with me on developing an initiative to teach kids in areas with heavy gang presence to be safe using social media."

He grinned. "Elle, that's fucking awesome. Congratulations. I'm proud of you."

My face warmed. "Thanks. I'm excited about it. This is a step in the right direction for sure."

"I'm really glad that you managed to make something good of last weekend."

"I liked spending that time with you, too." The words fell out of my mouth without thought. I almost slapped my palm over my lips, but I caught myself and did a weird flip thing with my hand before putting it on my lap. Blubbering idiot.

His brows arched. "Yeah?"

I looked down at my plate, hoping he wouldn't see my cheeks reddening, and nodded. "Yeah."

He grinned. "Me, too."

We finished dinner, then he insisted on doing the dishes. I made us tea and we sat on the couch and watched a few episodes of *Criminal Minds*. It was kind of our thing. At some point, I fell asleep and Keith carried me to bed.

SEVEN

KEITH

I took a swig of my beer while I sat at the bar watching the NY Rangers hockey game with a few of the guys from my firehouse. I'd suggested we check out this place called Varsity, apparently it was *the* spot to watch hockey on the West Side. Jace Palmer and Dylan Hogan had sent their wives on a girls' night, so we were free to have some guy time drinking beer and watching sports. Life was good.

And then Brielle walked in. Okay, fine. I admit I had chosen that place because she'd said she was going there on a date, but I still wasn't prepared to actually see her. She had on black skinny jeans with tan leather, knee-high boots and a white knit, off-the-shoulder slouchy sweater. Her tan leather jacket and Burberry scarf completed the look, and I had to admit she looked like she'd stepped out of a fashion magazine. Although, that was nothing new for her. The woman had a keen eye for fashion.

I watched as she stripped off her jacket and tucked her scarf into the sleeve before she hung it up on the back of the chair at the high-top table they were claiming. Her collar bones looked sexy as hell on display like that. I'd given up on fighting my desire for her. When I'd made dinner the night before, I'd planned on talking to her about going out with me on a date, but then she told me that she was going out with someone else and that put an end to that.

The past week had been brutal trying to fight my attraction for her. No matter how hard I'd tried, I couldn't get the memory of that kiss or the feel of her cuddled up against me in bed out of my mind. As much as I didn't want to fuck up our friendship, I also couldn't fight the fact that I wanted her. Bad.

She scooped her loosely curled dark hair behind her shoulder and her date—*Paul*—leaned down toward her ear and whispered something. I wanted to deck him for standing so close to her. What was wrong with me? Brielle and I had double dated before and I hadn't been jealous then, so why was I all of a sudden feeling very possessive of her? Two-and-a-half days as my fake girlfriend and I was done for.

This Paul guy was tall, but shorter than me and was on the lanky side. It got better: he had a man bun. I actually smacked my hand over my eyes.

"What's up, dude?" Jace asked.

I shook my head. "Nothing."

"Bullshit," Dylan interjected. "You look like you're gonna beat the crap out of someone." An accurate assumption.

"You know that girl I told you guys about the other night?" I'd confided in them at work. They were both married and I was feeling overwhelmingly at a loss for what to do, so I'd asked them for advice.

"Your roommate? The one you hooked up with last weekend?" Jace asked.

"I wouldn't say we hooked up. It was fake."

Dylan asked, "How'd she like the chicken parm? That gets me every time my wife makes it."

I didn't need to be reminded of my kitchen debacle. "Yeah, it was fine. But she's here."

They both spun their heads around.

"Where?"

"What's she wearing?"

I shook my head. "Please, make it more obvious." I took a sip from my beer bottle. "She's on a date."

Dylan patted my shoulder. "Tough break, man."

I watched as Paul made his way back from the bar carrying a beer and a glass of red wine, which he handed to her. I made a sound of disgust. "He has a man bun."

They both laughed.

"Ah, hell. You've still got a shot then, Hart," Jace replied.

I sighed. "I don't know if I want a shot."

Dylan narrowed his eyes. "Having a change of heart? Because that's not what you said on Tuesday."

I went back and forth by the minute as to whether or not I should pursue something more with Brielle. My dick sure as hell did, but the last thing I wanted to do was fuck up our friendship. "She's my roommate. What if we go down that path and everything gets screwed up? Then what?"

Jace tipped back his beer, then said, "Sure, that could very well happen, but it's a risk you've got to be willing to take if you think she's worth trying for."

Dylan knocked on the bar. "We need shots." He motioned to the bartender and ordered some Irish Whiskey.

Two shots and a beer later, I was feeling damn good. Well, other than the fact that I couldn't peel my eyes off of Brielle and her date. She'd been facing away from me the whole night, but from the expressions on his face, it seemed to be going well.

I ground my teeth when the guy put his hand on her thigh.

"I can't do this." I tilted my bottle back and drained it. Then I stood up.

"Dude, what are you doing?" Dylan asked.

"Just going to say hello." I swiped his beer off the bar and pushed through the crowd, ignoring my friends' attempts to stop me.

I waltzed right up to their table. "Elle, what a nice surprise."

Her mouth hung open. "Uh, Keith. Hi. What are you doing here?"

I pointed to my friends. "Watching the game with some of the guys from work." I turned to her date. "I'm a fireman." *Which means I'm way more badass than you, Mr. Man Bun.* I tilted my beer—well, Dylan's beer—toward him. "I'm Keith, by the way. Brielle and I live together."

The guy squirmed.

Brielle jumped in. "As roommates. Keith is my roommate. That's all."

I smiled at her—the kind that meant business—and said, "That's all." My tone said anything but.

She blushed. "You should go back to your friends, Keith. I'll see you at home."

Ouch. "Sorry, didn't mean to disturb your date. Surprised to see you here is all."

"Right..." she dragged out the vowel.

"Where are you from, Keith? I detect a southern accent," Man Bun asked.

He could hear my accent? *Fuck, I must be drunker than I thought.* I worked hard to conceal my Kentucky twang.

Brielle answered for me. "He's from Kentucky. And right now, he's going back to where he came from on that bar stool over there." She pointed across the room.

I covered my heart. "Why, Elle, if I didn't know any better,

I'd think you were tryin' to get rid of me. I simply saw y'all over here and thought I'd drop by and say hello."

She looked at Man Bun. "Would you excuse us a moment?" She hoped off her chair, grabbed my arm and dragged me back to the guys. "Pardon me, but I found a stray that I think belongs to you," she said to Dylan and Jace, which made them laugh. "He wandered right into the middle of my date, so maybe you can put a leash on him."

Jace was in stitches. "No sweat. We've got him."

"Thank you." She turned on her heels and went back to Man Bun.

I grumbled as Dylan pulled me down onto the stool.

"Seems like that went well," Dylan commented.

"Shut the fuck up," I hissed, then I took a sip of the beer that I'd commandeered from him. I switched to water after that.

By the third period of the game, I was over it. I'd sobered up and it was taking every ounce of my willpower to keep from staring at Brielle. "I'm heading out, guys." I threw some cash down on the bar, then fist-bumped them both on my way out. My eyes met Brielle's for a flash, but I forced myself to keep going.

Back at my apartment, I stripped down to my underwear, then put on a pair of shorts and I was going to put on a t-shirt, but changed my mind. I went out to the living room and plopped down on the couch to watch the end of the game. Part of me wanted Brielle to walk in with her date and have him see me sitting there half naked. I'd bet anything that his body was nothing compared to mine, but then I thought better of it, because if Brielle brought him home, then it meant the date had gone well, and while I wanted her to be happy, I didn't want her to be happy with anyone but me.

We'd danced around what had happened all week, but I

was tired of it. I knew what I'd felt and I was hard-pressed to believe that she hadn't felt it, too. At least a little. I kicked my feet up onto the coffee table and stared at the TV, pretty much counting the minutes as I waited for her to get home. When the game ended and she still wasn't back, I became restless.

Eleven o'clock at night was a good a time as any to do pushups, right? I got down on the floor of the living room and worked out my frustration. When I was two-hundred and something in, the door opened. I didn't stop or bother to look up as her heels tapped across the floor.

She crouched down beside my head. "What are you doing?"

"Pushups."

"No kidding. Why?"

"Felt...like...it."

Her hands went to my shoulder blades and I paused long enough for her to sit on my back. We'd done that before. I pushed out another set. When I stopped, she got off and I popped up onto my knees.

"How was your date?"

She sat down on the couch. "Fine. Care to tell me how you coincidentally wound up at the same bar?" I knew that she would call me on it.

I stood and put my hands on my hips. Her eyes dipped to my abs for a fleeting moment. "You said it was the place to go to watch the hockey game."

She unzipped her boots and discarded them on the floor before pulling her legs up and tucking them beneath her. "Is that it?"

I nodded, but refused to meet her gaze. "Yeah."

She let out a sigh. "Paul was kind of lame. Perfectly nice, but a bit boring."

My eyebrows shot up and I looked at her. "Oh?"

She shrugged. "Should we *talk*, Keith?"

My heart rate spiked. "Talk?"

"You made me dinner last night."

I tilted my head. "So?"

"You don't cook."

"I, I felt like trying," I stammered.

"You butted in on my date tonight like I belonged to you."

You do belong to me. "What can I say, I got a weird vibe from the guy. You can do better."

Her dark eyes stared silently into mine while she took several breaths. "You kissed me, Keith."

"I had to."

"No. Not like that you didn't."

This was it. The conversation we'd been dancing around for nearly a week. I didn't have the balls to bring it up, but apparently Brielle did. She stood and walked over to me.

When she was a foot away, tops, she whispered, "Why?"

My breathing shallowed. "I...I'm not sure," I lied.

Her lips tightened into a line. "We're friends."

"I know."

"Best friends."

"Yeah.

"Roommates."

"Yes."

She crossed her arms. "We were supposed to fake that kiss."

I sighed. "I know."

Her dark eyes had locked with mine and I was powerless to look away. "But we didn't."

I shook my head the slightest bit. "No."

She swallowed. "Is this going to be a problem?"

She was passing me the puck. I could keep lying and try to move on like nothing had happened. Or I could tell her the truth and risk everything. Jace's words echoed in my head, *it's a risk you've got to be willing to take if you think she's worth trying for.* Brielle was worth it. She was already special to me. Maybe, just maybe, we wouldn't fuck it all up. Maybe we'd make it that much better.

My mouth had dried up. I opened and closed it several times, while I considered my response.

She was patient.

Finally, I said, "It doesn't have to be."

She rolled her lips together. "How's that?"

I reached for her hand—something I'd done for years without it being weird—but since the previous weekend, that had changed. Holding her slender fingers between mine, I whispered, "Maybe we could be more."

"More?" she whispered back.

"I hadn't expected that kiss either, you know. But I haven't been able to stop thinking about it. Can you honestly tell me that you didn't feel it, too?" I lobbed the puck back at her.

Her chest rose and fell as she took several heavy breaths. "I felt it."

Hallelujah. A knot in the pit of my stomach released and I brought my other hand up, smoothed it over her cheek, and cupped the side of her face.

Her mouth opened a sliver while her dark eyes remained fixed on mine.

"What if..." I let the question hang between us.

This time, she was the one who stuttered. "I...I don't know."

I lowered my face toward her. "Then maybe we should find out." I paused with my mouth hovering just above her lips. I wasn't going to make my move until I knew she was fine with it.

It felt like forever before she uttered, "Okay."

My mouth fell to hers and this time, without an audience, I didn't hold back. She released my fingers and her arms wrapped around my back, while I brought my hand to the back of her neck. Her lips were still slightly chilled from having been outside, and they felt so dang perfect as I caged one between mine. My tongue ached to taste her, so it darted out and met hers in the middle. Together they danced, as I took her lip deeper inside.

She moaned against me and it spoke directly to my cock, which started rousing to attention. My fingers went into her thick hair while her palms dipped down my back, over my hips, and up my abdomen before landing on my bare chest. Every nerve that had fired the other night on the staircase fired again, but ten-fold.

Any doubts I'd had melted away. Brielle was where I was meant to be. She was mine. Always had been. It just took us a while to realize that, but now that I had, I'd never let her go. I bit down playfully on her lip and the sound she made sent a shiver up my spine. Her fingers went to my hips and she pulled, smashing my growing erection against her. Fuck, I wanted her. Right there in the living room. I wanted to bend her over the couch and bury myself inside of her while I gripped her ass and made her scream for more.

I stepped her back until we were by the couch, then I sat down on it and took her with me, making her straddle my lap. I clutched her hips while she ground against me, and my tongue lapped against hers. Her hands were on my chest; on my shoulders; up my neck; in my hair. She moved frantically, her desperation matching my own. I needed more. I needed her.

"Elle," I murmured against her lips. We had to stop before we took things too far, too soon.

She purred.

I thrust my hips up.

She hummed.

I thrust again.

My cock was painfully hard and in desperate need of attention. As badly as I wanted to give it to him, my mind was fighting a war with my body.

I dug my fingers into her hips, pinning her to me.

I wanted her with everything I had, but we couldn't cross that line yet. I'd never forgive myself for taking us there before we were truly ready.

But the heat building where her pussy was smashed against me was begging for more. And fuck, I wanted to give it to her, but once we had sex, our friendship would never be able to come back from that. We needed to be sure we wanted to go there first because Brielle wouldn't be a casual lay. If my heart had anything to say about it, she was the top contender for my forever.

And I would not fuck that up because of my cock.

I slowed the pace of our kiss and then eased my mouth away from hers. "Elle."

Her eyes had darkened with lust, and they stared into mine with just as much amazement as I was feeling. I brushed the hair from the side of her face and planted a kiss on her cheek. I clamped my eyelids shut. "If we don't stop now..."

"I know. You're right." She leaned her forehead against mine. "Keith, that was...hell, I don't even know how to describe it."

"Me neither," I whispered before my lids fluttered open.

She pulled her head back and stared at me. "Are we? Are we doing this?"

"I know I want to. Do you?"

She sucked her bottom lip into her mouth and I desperately wanted to kiss her again. She nodded. "I think I do."

My heart leapt. "I'm working tomorrow, but Sunday, I'd really like to take you on a date. A real one."

She smiled.

I smiled back. "Will you go on a date with me, Brielle Jackson?"

She giggled. "Yes, Keith Hart. I will."

I pulled her to me and kissed her.

BRIELLE

I slipped into my black cocktail dress and danced around until I could reach the zipper, then tugged it up. Keith was taking me on a date. An actual date. Not as friends. I didn't know where to, but he'd told me to get dressed up, and I was more than happy to oblige. While I struggled by the minute over whether or not dating Keith was a good idea, I was too giddy to stop it from happening.

When I'd gotten home from my date the other night, I hadn't intended for things to go the way that they had. After seeing Keith's behavior at the bar in front of Paul, I knew we had to talk because pretending like nothing had changed hadn't stopped the fact that things had indeed changed between us, but I honestly hadn't expected him to kiss me again. And holy hell did he kiss me!

The things he'd made my body feel had made that kiss we'd shared on the staircase at his parents' seem like child's play. Running my hands over the ridges of his abs and his strong chest had sent shockwaves directly to my groin. Straddling his lap with his hard bulge pressed against me had nearly sent me over the edge. When he'd stopped us, I'd wanted to cry out in protest, but he had done the right thing. Despite how badly I'd wanted him, it would've been a mistake. One step at a time.

I was fishing my favorite red stilettos out of my closet when there was a faint knocking sound. Backing out of the closet, I listened closer, and heard it again. Someone was knocking on our apartment door. I opened the door to my bedroom and poked my head out. "Keith, can you get that?" I slipped one foot into my shoe.

Another knock.

"Keith?"

No response. *Where was he?* I slid on my other shoe and crossed our apartment to the door. Upon opening it, my jaw dropped.

Keith was standing there in a gray tailored suit, sans tie, the top button on his white shirt open showing off that sexy dip in his throat. His typically tousled fawn-colored hair was combed, parted to the side, and styled to perfection, just as it had been at the party. And he was holding a bouquet of red roses.

My smile was so big it threatened to crack the corners of my mouth. "Keith, what are you—"

"I'm picking you up for our date."

I giggled.

"These are for you." He handed me the roses, which I happily took.

"Thank you. This is very sweet of you."

"Can I come in?"

I played along. "Please do, I'm almost ready."

I stepped aside to let him pass, but instead of walking by me, he stopped to give me a gentle kiss on the cheek first. I closed the door and followed him into our apartment.

"This is a nice place, you've got," he said as he looked around like he hadn't lived there for seven years.

I placed the roses down on the kitchen island while I searched the cabinets for a vase. "I can't take the credit. My roommate did the decorating."

"I think I'm going to like her."

I stifled a laugh. "Him, actually."

"Oh?" His brows raised as he picked a picture frame up off of the bookshelf. It was a photo of us from his firehouse picnic that past summer. "This the guy?"

I nodded, fighting laughter. "Yes, it is."

He sucked in his cheeks. "I'm going to have to meet him. Make sure he knows that you're off limits." He smirked.

I found a vase and stretched up, but it was just out of my reach. Without having to be asked, Keith reached over the top of me and grabbed it, then set it down on the counter. He smelled delicious. Like an Armani model. Not that I spent much time—or any time—around Armani models, but I assumed that they smelled all masculine and expensive-like.

"Off limits, huh?" I responded as I filled the vase with water.

He came up behind me at the sink and put his hands on my hips. A chill shot through me at his touch. He leaned into the side of my neck and whispered against my skin, "I don't intend to share you." The heat of his breath made the tiny hairs rise up and I flinched from the pleasure.

I turned off the water and whispered. "I'm all yours."

His lips connected with the top of my collarbone, making me whimper. "Good," he growled before releasing my hips and stepping back.

I fought the urge to press the vase against my chest to cool off from the heat he'd worked up in me.

He removed the roses from the plastic and began to open the drawer to get the scissors, but stopped himself and stepped aside. "Where are your scissors?"

I failed to stifle my laugh as I pointed to the drawer he had started opening. Once he retrieved the scissors, he cut the bottoms off of the stems over the sink and placed the flowers into the vase. Then, he scooped up the stems and stepped on the pedal of the garbage, depositing them in there. He moved the vase to the center of the island.

"Perfect," I said, although I wasn't just talking about the flowers. "I'll go grab my purse and we can go...wherever it is we are going."

He smirked. "Sounds good."

I went to walk away, but he called out and stopped me. "Brielle?" It was weird hearing my full name come from his mouth.

"Yes?" I turned.

His eyes scanned me from head to toe. "You look incredible."

I blushed. "So do you." Then, I turned and went to my room. I took a few steadying breaths as I grabbed my red Tory Burch clutch, the one that perfectly matched my shoes, off of my bed before returning to the living room.

He was leaning against the island with his ankles crossed and his hands in his pockets looking all sexy like he owned the place. I mean, he did own the place, but I'm talking about that kind of total confidence. Nothing sexier. "Shall we?" His smile sent a jolt to my lady parts.

"Absolutely. Are you going to tell me where we're going?"

We made our way to the entryway and Keith took my coat out of the closet, helping me into it, before retrieving his own. "It's a surprise." He opened the door, placed his hand on the small of my back to guide me out, then closed and locked it behind us.

The sun was already setting by the time we got downstairs, but the city lights were wonderful at night although I hated that it would be totally dark by four-thirty. The doorman flagged down a taxi for us and we slid into the back. Keith slipped a piece of paper through the seat divider to the driver, "Can you take us here, please?" Apparently, he was intent on keeping it a surprise.

He swung his arm around my shoulders and tugged me to him—his warm body welcoming in the cold. The driver took us through midtown which was buzzing with activity. Tourism was always busy in Manhattan, but particularly so during the holidays. The decorations and holiday lights on the streets and the buildings made for quite a sight. After a short drive we pulled up to Radio City Music Hall and the cab came to a stop.

For the second time in the space of half an hour, my jaw dropped. "Keith, did you?"

The smile he gave me warmed me on the inside. "You said you'd always wanted to be a Rockette."

The Radio City Christmas Spectacular was one of my absolute favorite things. Period. I'd been a dancer growing up and I'd always dreamed of dancing on that stage in the Christmas show. I loved going and tried to see it every December, but I'd got caught up and hadn't gotten tickets in time this year.

Keith paid the driver and got out, then held his hand out to assist me.

"How did you even get tickets? Weekends have been sold out for weeks."

He knew how upset I'd been about it because I'd sulked around our apartment for a solid three days. He shrugged. "I have connections."

I laughed. Of course, the son of a senator would be able to make that happen. I suppose I probably could've gotten press access, but going with Keith was a much better idea.

I clutched his arm as we pushed through the entrance.

We'd arrived forty-five minutes before curtain and the lobby was already jampacked with people. Clutching my hand, Keith weaved us through the crowd and brought me to a door marked *Staff Only*. He showed something on his phone to the guard outside who then relayed the information over his headset. Moments later, a woman came through the door.

"Mr. Hart?"

He stuck out his free hand—the one not holding mine—and shook hers. "Yes. And this is Brielle Jackson."

I had to let go of Keith to shake her hand, but he promptly took it back. I kinda liked it. And by kinda, I mean a lot.

"Come on back," she said, while holding the door open for us.

I looked up at Keith, but all he gave me was a smile and a wiggle of his brows. We were ushered into a room that looked like rehearsal space, and the woman told us to wait there.

"What's this?" I asked him.

"You'll see."

I elbowed him. "You're killing me, Hart."

He winked. "Worth it, Jackson."

The door opened and in walked five of the legendary Rockettes. My jaw dropped for the third time inside an hour.

"You must be Brielle," one of the women said.

I nodded.

"We heard you've always wanted to audition for this show."

My eyes darted to Keith, before turning my attention back to her. "I'm half an inch too short."

"How about we teach you a combination?"

My hand went to my chest. "Seriously?"

"Absolutely." She smiled.

"I'd love that." I spent the next ten minutes learning a part of the kick line in their opening number to Jingle Bells. It was spectacular. No pun intended. When we were finished, they took photos with me and Keith and then had to go get set for the show.

Once they were gone, I wrapped my arms around Keith and stared up at him. "Thank you. That was an experience I'll never forget."

"That smile on your face is all the thanks I need."

The woman who'd brought us back there returned. "Allow me to show you to your seats Mr. Hart, Ms. Jackson."

We followed her through a stage door to the orchestra. Keith had gotten us seats in the front row on the aisle. He insisted I take the aisle seat and we settled in for the show. I was so excited I could cry.

I turned toward him as the lights dimmed. "Keith?"

"Yeah, Elle?"

I kissed him. It was a chaste kiss, but feeling his lips even for a moment, was all I needed. It was all I'd ever need. The happiness brewing in my core told me just as much. The show started and he laced his fingers with mine.

It was magical. Nothing was more representative to me of Christmas than the Rockettes. During their "Here Comes Santa Claus" number, they came down the aisle beside me and I understood why Keith had wanted me to have the aisle seat. When the show ended, I teared up as we gave them a standing ovation. Despite the fact I'd seen the show countless times, none of them topped this.

Keith led me outside and handed his phone to someone to take our picture beneath the marquee, then we walked up a block and Keith hailed us a cab. Seven minutes later we arrived at 230 5th.

We rode the elevator up to the roof. I'd heard of their rooftop igloos, but I'd never been. That was about to change. Normally, their igloos were first come, first served, but apparently Keith had leveraged his family name again. I wasn't complaining. They escorted us directly to one of their heated igloos.

"Are you freaking kidding me?" I exclaimed.

His smile lit up his entire face. "Cool, huh?"

"This is...beyond cool." The clear dome was adorned with a multitude of colored LEDs. Surrounded by the lights of Manhattan skyscrapers, it couldn't get much more enchanting. The igloos were made for more than two people, but Keith must've worked his magic to reserve it for us alone.

The menu at 230 5th was nothing special. It was the kind of place people went for the ambiance rather than the culinary experience. The server came and Keith ordered us a bottle of Bordeaux and two burgers; he knew how much I loved burgers. The simple kind, not the fancy gourmet, over-the-top kind.

I felt like I was living a dream. "Keith, how did you manage this?"

"There are perks to being Lemon and Senator Hart's son. My family is connected."

That much I knew. "Well, thank you. This is truly wonderful."

He reached across the table and grasped my hand. "Anything for you."

The server returned and poured us each a glass of wine.

Keith held his up. "To exploring possibilities."

I grinned and clinked my glass to his before taking a sip.

"Did you enjoy the show?"

Laughter forced out powered by my diaphragm. "Enjoyed it? No. That was the greatest show I've ever seen. Thanks to you."

His eyes sparkled. "Do you know how beautiful you are when you smile?"

I blushed.

He squeezed my hand. "Is it weird that this doesn't feel weird?"

I knew exactly what he meant. "Yes. But I also think that's a very good thing."

"Elle, I think we can make this work."

God, I hoped so. I couldn't bear the thought of losing him. I nodded. "Perhaps we can."

He told me all about his shift the day before and I listened intently while he detailed how they had responded to an accident involving one of those Chinatown tour buses. One thing was clear: Keith loved his job. Being a firefighter meant everything to him, and I swallowed the thought of his parents trying to make him give all of that up. If they couldn't see how passionate their son was about his career, then they were utterly blind. Not an appealing quality in a potential future president.

Our burgers arrived and I wasted no time digging in. I was hungry. It wasn't the best burger I'd ever had, but it was far from being the worst.

Keith took a bite of his and once he swallowed, he said, "I was thinking we need a Christmas tree."

"Oh, do we?"

"Yeah. What kind of Christmas would it be without a tree?"

I shrugged. "We can probably order one online."

He paused with his burger mid-air. "Please tell me you did not just suggest we get an artificial tree off of the internet."

I smirked. "Not good enough for you?"

He shook his head. "We need a real tree."

I tapped the table with my fingers. "If you want to take care of it, by all means, let's get a real tree."

"Done. When?"

"When?"

"Yes. When can you get off so we can go upstate and chop down a tree?"

I nearly spit out my wine. "You want to actually cut down your own tree?"

He eyed me like I had five heads. "It's the only way."

"But there are plenty of nice, pre-cut trees at the tree markets throughout the city."

He snorted. "That's cheating."

I sipped my Bordeaux. "If that's what you want to do."

"Yes. When?"

"Where upstate would we be going? Like is it close enough for us to go when I get off work?"

He bit his lip. "I'll have to figure that out."

"Get back to me on that and we'll plan something."

He stole a fry off my plate.

"Hey! You have your own."

He smirked. "But yours are better."

My eyes widened and I did my best to stare him down all intimidating-like. "People have been killed for worse."

He leaned across the table and whispered, "Good luck, Elle." Then he stole another fry.

I grabbed one off his plate and threw it at him.

"Oh, you want to play it that way, huh?"

I reached for his wine glass and drained it.

He pursed his lips. "Is that so?"

I placed the empty glass back down in front of him. "Apparently what's yours is mine."

His tongue swiped between his lips and then he bit down on the bottom one. "I have something you can have." The black of his pupils overtook the copper in his irises.

I slid my finger slowly over the edge of my sweetheart neckline and his eyes dipped to my chest to follow the trail. "Do you now?"

"Come here," he ordered, his already deep voice plummeted an octave.

I made him sweat it out a beat before I stood and glided around to his side of the table. When I got to him, he pulled me down onto his lap and I slung an arm around his neck, while he cradled my back with one of his. His arousal was unmistakable and I desperately wanted to feel what was beneath the fabric. Keith reached for his water glass and drank it down to the ice. When he discarded the glass, he opened his mouth and showed me the ice cube trapped between his teeth. I shivered at the though of what he might do with that.

In a swift movement he traced my cleavage with the cube, then released it between my breasts, letting the ice fall down my dress. I gasped and tried to jump up, but he held me to him and gripped the back of my head, pulling my mouth to his. His lips were frozen from the ice and I was shivering from this game of his.

He sucked hard on my lips, which tingled from the temperature and the pressure of his kiss. I hummed against him and he took my mouth harder, letting his tongue slip inside. I quickly forgot about the cold water dripping from my breasts down my stomach. The ice seemed to awaken something in me. This carnal desire boiled up and I weaved my fingers into his hair and tugged.

If we kept it up any longer, we'd end up in a jail cell for indecent exposure on a rooftop bar in the middle of Manhattan. I tugged harder on his hair to break our seal and forced myself to pull my head back as well. We both panted and he stared deep into my eyes with a look that said he wanted more. And dammit, so did I.

I got off his lap and returned to my chair where I casually began putting on my scarf, gloves, and coat.

He took my lead and stuck his head out of the igloo to call

for the server. When the guy approached, Keith immediately handed him his credit card and said something that I couldn't hear, but judging by the speed with which the server disappeared, I imagined it was some kind of encouragement to get the guy to hurry. He returned less than a minute later. Keith signed the bill and put on his coat, then grabbed my hand and dragged me to the elevator. We rode down with a crowd of people and it killed me to not be able to continue what we'd started.

Once on the sidewalk, Keith immediately stepped into the street and held up his hand, getting a cab to stop. We slid into the back and he gave the driver our address. Keith must've been as eager as I was because he grabbed my face and brought me in for another kiss. Our hands attempted to explore each other's bodies through the thick layers we had on, but we didn't get very far with that.

Until Keith found an opening at the hem of my dress and slipped his fingers between my thighs. I inhaled sharply as he massaged over my tights. Like his kiss, he wasn't gentle as he grabbed onto my muscle, making me clench my legs together. His hand slid further up, forcing my legs to part for him. I was vaguely aware that we had an audience, but I couldn't care less. I wanted Keith all over my body, and I couldn't wait any longer.

My tongue traced over his lip and he groaned, "Elle." Then he sucked my lip between his just as his fingers reached my center.

I let out a poorly stifled moan as two of his fingertips pet me through my panties.

He dragged his mouth away and went straight for my earlobe, biting down on it and then releasing. He whispered, "You're so fucking wet for me."

"Yes," I whispered back as he sucked on my neck.

The driver punched the brake and slammed on his horn,

interrupting us. Probably for the best because at the rate we were going, things would've escalated quickly and I knew that neither of us wanted to end up front page news for acting like horny teenagers in a taxi.

Keith eased his fingers out from between my legs and we both sat back. He held his hand out, palm up, and I placed mine in it. We avoided looking at each other the rest of the way home because I was certain that one look would've sent us straight down the path we'd been on. Thankfully, it didn't take too much longer for us to return to our apartment.

Keith paid the driver then yanked me out by my hand and we scurried into the building. We took the elevator up to our floor with an elderly couple and the entire time Keith held my hand so tightly I thought it might break. Or maybe it was me that was squeezing his that hard, I don't know.

At the door, he fumbled with his keys, trying the one to his storage locker first before realizing it wasn't even the same color as the house key. Once the door was open, he shoved me through it, then slammed it behind us. He made quick work of his coat, so I did the same, and we discarded them on the floor in the entryway. He grasped my arms and spun me around, pinning my back to the wall and holding me there with his hips.

He stared into my eyes. "Elle, I—"

I held my finger up to his lips. "Shh. Kiss me."

And he did.

I worked his suit jacket off of his shoulders and tugged it down his arms, then I yanked his shirt out of his pants and felt for the buttons.

He was grinding up against me, letting me feel how hard he was, and I nearly gave up on the buttons and ripped the shirt off of him out of desperate need. He clawed at the hem of my dress and lifted it above my hips, leaving only my tights and my panties between us. I worked apart the final button on his shirt and he swiftly rid himself of the material. My hands went up his sleeveless undershirt. My fingertips mauled his six pack. There was nothing sexier than those abdominal ripples.

His hand went between my legs, wasting no time finding my center. I moaned into his mouth. Seconds later I heard tearing and then felt his skin against my bare thighs where my tights had been a moment earlier. His fingers cupped my sex and I leaned into him as his mouth began urgently kissing across my collarbone.

"Fuck, your panties are soaked."

I bit down on my lip as he nibbled over my shoulder and I made quick work of his belt. Then the button. Then the zipper.

Before I could pull his pants down, he surprised me by lifting me up by the back of my thighs and making me wrap my legs around his hips, then he carried me to the couch. He laid me down and got on top of me, nestling his hips between my thighs. I tilted my pelvis so I could feel his sizable arousal against me. His tongue sought out mine and I whimpered as he ground against my saturated panties. I needed him. Badly.

I was about to tell him just that when we heard the toilet flush. We both jumped up.

"Stay here," he ordered, as he zipped and buttoned his pants, then crept across the kitchen toward the bathroom in the hall.

Someone was in our apartment. We'd left the lamp on in the living room, like we always did, that way we wouldn't come home to complete darkness so at least we could see our surroundings. My heart thumped as I pulled my dress down and slipped off my shoes so I could creep silently across to the front door and fish my phone out of my discarded purse to call the police.

I was halfway to the door, when I heard a high-pitched

scream followed by Keith's deep voice shouting, "What the fuck, Mother?"

"Language, darling. You gave me quite a fright."

Lemon Hart was here in our apartment?

"I gave you a fright? What are you doing in my apartment?" Keith sounded pissed.

My first inclination was to hide. I had no doubt that my lipstick was smeared all over my face, my hair was a disaster, and my tights hung in tatters down my legs. I ran for the door, picked up my jacket, and had my hand on the door knob when I heard her. "Oh, I did not realize you had company."

Busted.

I rubbed the back of my hand over my mouth and took a second to run my fingers through my hair before I turned around. Strategically, I let my jacket hang from my hands in front of me, blocking my legs.

I forced a smile. "Mrs. Hart. This is a surprise."

She made no attempt to hide her dissatisfaction with my appearance as she took me in with her eyes. "It was very last minute. Graham and I are in town for the evening and I thought I would swing by and say hello to my son."

Keith ran a hand down his face. I'd done a number on his hair. It was sticking up in all directions. "You let yourself into my apartment." It was a reprimand, not a question, but his mother waved him off.

"Well, I tried to call you, but when you did not pick up, I decided to drop in. You did not answer the door and I needed to use the facilities, so I used my key. I only just arrived a few minutes ago." She glanced at the floor where we'd discarded our clothing in a heap.

I looked at Keith, at a loss for what to do. The fury in his eyes was something I'd never seen before.

Mrs. Hart continued. "It appears I am interrupting something." For a woman who had let us sleep in the same bed under her roof—insisted upon it actually—she sounded entirely too judgmental. I suppose she realized I was clutching my coat because her next words were, "Or are you leaving, sugar?"

"Uhh," was all that came out.

Keith stepped in. "No, she's not leaving. She lives here."

His mother spun on her heels to face him. "What?" she exclaimed. A smile brightened up her face. "You two have moved in together?"

Maybe, while she wasn't looking at me, I could slowly back out the door and run. At a glacial pace, I reached behind me for the door knob.

Keith looked to me for help, but I stared back at him as if to say, *sorry, but you're on your own.*

"Yes, Brielle and I live together."

My fingers connected with the metal and I began to turn.

Mrs. Hart performed a series of mini claps in rapid succession. "Oh, darling this is wonderful."

Almost there. I could feel the latch retreating into the door.

She turned to me. "Brielle, you must come here so we can celebrate this momentous news."

So close...

"Actually, Mrs. Hart, I'm not feeling great. I think I'm just going to lay down." No way in hell was I going to stand next to Senator Hart's wife—Keith's *mom*—while wearing ripped tights. I stuck to the perimeter of the room as I skirted around her and Keith toward the bedrooms. "It was nice seeing you again."

"I hope you feel better, sugar. You absolutely must come for Christmas. Now that you and Keith are cohabitating, you might as well be family. I simply will not take no for an answer."

"Christmas. Sure," I blurted out in my haste, immediately regretting it.

"Fabulous."

I made it to the hall and went left toward my bedroom.

"Brielle," she called out. "Did you and Keith move into the other bedroom?"

My eyes widened. Keith's bedroom was on the opposite side of the hall. I tried to laugh it off. "Oh, you're right this is the wrong direction. I'm feeling a bit dizzy. The wine we had at dinner has gone straight to my head. I must have gotten disoriented." To Keith's bedroom I went.

I closed the door behind me and leaned against it as I let out a deep breath. *That was close.* I'd only been in Keith's room once or twice before and it felt wrong being in there without him, but I wasn't going anywhere until his mother was gone. I glanced around trying to figure out what to do with myself while I waited. God-knows how long Lemon Hart could impose herself on her son. I sat down on the edge of the bed, really wishing I had thought to grab my purse so I'd have my phone. Although, I hadn't predicted I'd be in Keith's room where I'd need it.

It felt deeply personal being in his space and I didn't want to seem nosey by peeking around. After a solid ten minutes of staring at my lap, I decided to lay down and wait for Keith to come get me.

I must've dozed off because the next thing I could recall was Keith sitting on the bed beside me, brushing the hair off of my forehead and whispering, "Elle?"

I begrudgingly opened my eyes. One thing I hated was being woken up.

"She's gone."

Who's gone? And then I remembered. A second later I also remembered I was in his bed, so I popped up. "I'm sorry. I guess I fell asleep waiting for you."

He gave me the most tender smile. "That's all right. I

wasn't going to wake you, but I figured you'd be much more comfortable if you changed out of that dress."

I glanced down at my cocktail dress. *That's right, we'd been on a date.* "That's probably a good idea." I stood up, feeling awkward.

Keith stood as well. He ran the back of his fingers along the side of my face, then kissed my forehead. "I'm sorry our night was ruined."

I shook my head. "It wasn't. I had an incredible time. Thank you."

He grinned. "Yeah? Me, too."

I pointed to the door. "I should go to bed. I've got to be up at four-thirty for work." I had no idea what time it was, but it had already been past my bed time when we'd gotten home.

"Of course."

Stepping around him, I headed for the door. I was nearly at my bedroom when I heard him behind me. "There's just one last thing."

I spun around. "What do you mean?"

"I have to walk you to your door after our first date like a gentleman." He smirked.

I giggled and pointed to my room. "Well, this is me."

"I'd really like to see you again, Brielle."

My stomach fluttered. "I'd like to see you again, too."

He smiled. "I'll call you tomorrow."

I grinned. "Sounds good."

He took a step toward me. "Can I give you a kiss good night?"

I bit down on my lip and nodded. He cupped my cheek and brought his lips tenderly to mine. This kiss was sweet—the kind that set the butterflies loose—rather than urgent and dripping with need. It only lasted a few seconds and then he pulled away and whispered, "Good night, Elle."

"Good night."

He let go of my cheek and went back to his bedroom, leaving me standing at my door with a smile on my face that I suspected wouldn't go away any time soon. I sighed as I entered my room. That was hands down the best first date I'd ever been on, and I was eager to get to sleep so I could wake up and see him again.

NINE

KEITH

It'd been three days since my date with Brielle and I was still riding the high. I honestly couldn't have asked for it to have gone any better. Well, save for the part where I'd been cock blocked by my mother's surprise appearance. That being said, it had probably been for the best. With the way that Brielle and I had been carrying on, I would've had sex with her, and it would've probably still been too soon for that.

When I pulled up to the USBC news studio, she was already standing out front looking cute as hell in her long, burgundy down coat with the fur-trimmed hood held snug against her face. I hadn't seen her since our date because of how our work schedules had conflicted. She had left Monday before I'd gotten up and then I had left for my twenty-four-hour shift before she'd gotten home. I hadn't returned home until Tuesday night and she'd had a dinner with some people at the network, so she'd come home after I'd been asleep. Again, that morning, she had been gone before I'd woken. It was almost like we were dating for real instead of living under the same roof. I'd even called her from work the next day to tell her what a great time I'd had.

She scampered to the car, hopped in and shivered. "So. Cold."

"Why didn't you wait inside, crazy?"

I'd turned the seat warmer on for her before I'd arrived so that it would be hot when I got there. She wiggled her butt as she settled in. "Guess I didn't realize how cold it was."

It was a particularly chilly day with a real-feel of eighteen degrees. And we were driving an hour north of the city to cut down a Christmas tree. Perhaps we could've planned around the weather better, but we were running out of days if we wanted to have a tree before the holiday.

I merged onto the Hudson Parkway, which ran parallel to the Hudson River on the New Jersey side of Manhattan. We were going to a tree farm in Yorktown Heights, a small town in the northern part of Westchester County by the Putnam County border. I'd asked around the firehouse and a few of the guys with kids had recommended it.

Brielle placed her hands over the heat vents on the dash. "Why is it so cold?"

I laughed. "How are you surprised? I watched the weather report on *your* show like an hour ago."

She scrunched her face up. "Very funny. And what *you* don't see on *my* show is the part during the weather where I'm flipping through the next segment's notes or drinking my water or listening to my producer in my earpiece about some breaking news."

"Hmm. I had no idea."

"Maybe you should get your facts straight before you go poking fun at someone then, Hart," she said playfully with a grin.

"Duly noted, Jackson."

"How far is this place anyway?" she asked.

I checked my GPS. "About fifty minutes." The benefit of going in the middle of the afternoon was that hopefully traffic would be at a minimum. Well, for New York anyway. That was one thing I missed about Kentucky. I'd never known traffic until we had moved to D.C. and New York was equally as bad.

She groaned. "And you're sure we can't just go pick up a tree from a market in the city?"

Brielle had never cut down her own tree and for some unexplainable reason, I felt compelled to experience that with her. I had fond memories of going out on my grandparents' land with my brother and finding a tree every year when we were young. That had stopped when we'd moved into the Governor's Mansion because there was an entire staff that took care of the decorating.

"Yes, I'm sure. It'll be fun. We'll go for a sleigh ride and drink hot chocolate and find the perfect tree for our place." *Our* place. The connotation of that had changed entirely in less than a week. Brielle and I were roommates, but since we started dating, I guess that meant we were living together. Big difference.

She sighed. "If you insist on turning me into an icicle, I am going to hold you personally responsible for warming me up when we are through."

I smirked. "Gladly. I'll keep you warm anytime, just say the word." Out of the corner of my eye I caught her glance at me with a devilish grin.

For the rest of the ride, we caught each other up on what we'd missed over the past few days. I shared details about a few of the runs I'd gone on at work and she told me about what was happening at the studio. Having been friends for so long, we'd built a natural rapport. I'd been worried that it would change after we went out, but I was thrilled to learn that it hadn't.

As I pulled down the dirt road to get to the farm it started snowing. There was something about getting a Christmas tree in the snow that was reminiscent of a fairytale.

Brielle sighed. "I'm holding you to that keeping me warm thing we were talking about."

"Like I said, anytime."

"Mmm hmm. Remember that when my frozen toes are shocking your skin later."

Thoughts of being naked with Brielle swam around my mind making me chub up. After we parked, I discreetly adjusted my dick before we went anywhere. Once we were both out of the car, I pulled Brielle into my arms. "I've missed you, Elle."

She smiled. "Yeah. Me, too."

"You missed you?" I jested.

She rolled her eyes. "You know what I mean."

"So, technically this is our second date."

She nodded and hummed in agreement.

"And there's something I've been dying to do since the other night."

"Oh?" Her brows lifted.

I gripped her chin with my hand and tilted her face up. "Yeah." I bent toward her and took claim of her mouth, while the fur on her hood tickled my forehead. To start, I was gentle as my lips told her how much she meant to me, but then I became more insistent as I probed my tongue in looking for hers, telling her exactly how much I'd missed her. She melted into me and I held her close, then slowed our kiss and pulled away, leaving both of us a little breathless.

I placed a kiss on the tip of her nose, which was starting to chill. "Thank you."

"For what?"

"For indulging my need."

She smirked. "Oh, I needed it, too."

I released her and held out my hand. "Shall we?"

She laced her gloved fingers with mine and followed me to the sleighs. They were pulled by tractors rather than horses, which was mildly disappointing, but being able to wrap my arm around her and hold her close more than made up for it even though our bulky jackets got in the way. They dropped us off in the middle of the plantation where rows of Douglas and Fraser Firs stood tall waiting to find homes for Christmas. The snow dusted their branches, heightening their beauty, and it was incredibly peaceful. Even Brielle seemed to have forgotten about the cold as we milled about looking for the perfect tree while inhaling the intoxicating scent of pine.

For as resistant as she had been to the idea, once there, Brielle was all-in. I picked out a few, which she studied intensely before saying no because it was *too sparse* or *too fat* or *asymmetrical* or *not conical enough*. After about fifteen minutes of carting around a bow saw, we came upon a tree that made us both stop in our tracks. It stood just over six feet and the bluish-green needles of the Fraser Fir glistened as the sunlight reflected off of the snow flakes nestled in its branches.

Brielle moved first and she surged toward it squealing with glee. "This is it!" She reminded me of a child on Christmas morning and that was the moment I realized I wanted a future with her. A real future. I wanted to be sipping tea around our tree as the kids came charging into the room with contagious laughter at the sight of the presents Santa had left them. Brielle would take pictures while I helped unbox all of the toys once they were unwrapped. I'd glance over at my wife and smile, which she'd return with one of her own—one that said how lucky we were to have our little family.

"Keith." She clapped her hands to get my attention. "Stop staring at me all goofy and come caveman this tree down."

I shook the vision from my head and got down on my stomach before reaching under the branches with the saw. By the time it finally tumbled to the ground, I had a whole new appreciation for the power tools we used at work. I reached between the branches, gripping the trunk, and stood the tree up.

"Let's do it," I said as I carried it toward the sleighs with Brielle behind me.

"You sure you don't need help?" She must've asked me a dozen times.

"Elle, compared to what I do for a living, carrying this tree is a piece of cake."

We waited for an empty sleigh and when it arrived the farmhand hooked the tree to the back on a toboggan. Brielle cuddled against me. "You were right. This was fun."

I played like I was reaching into my jacket for my phone. "Can you say that one more time? I'd like to record it for future use."

She pinched my thigh. "Nice try."

When we got back to the barn, the staff wrapped our tree up in protective netting while we went inside for hot chocolate. Brielle clutched the paper cup to her face, closed her eyes and breathed deep. The tip of her nose was red, as were her ears, but she hadn't complained about the cold. Still, I was looking forward to getting her home and warming her up. I had a few more surprises up my sleeve.

While she used the restroom, I hastened through the gift shop to look for an ornament. When I found the perfect one, I rushed to pay for it and slipped it into my coat pocket a second before she appeared.

"Ready?"

She nodded.

I pulled the car up and fastened the tree to my roof rack.

Once it was secure, we headed back to the city. I fantasized about waking up with Brielle on Christmas morning and having breakfast by our tree. One thing I could cook was pancakes—the boxed kind, anyway, but I always put blueberries or chocolate chips in them to make them fancy.

Then I realized, Brielle and I had never discussed Christmas. I had to remedy that. "What are your plans for Christmas?"

"No plans. My parents are going to be in London, but I can't get enough time off to make the trip." A hint of sadness clouded her voice. "You're going to Kentucky, right?"

Shit. I'd somehow forgotten about that. "That's the plan, but you can't be alone on Christmas. Maybe I can stay."

She placed her hand on my arm that was resting on the center console. "No, Keith. You have to be with your family on Christmas."

But you are my family. In a way, she had been for a while. I was a believer in being able to choose your family. Family was someone who you could be yourself around; someone who would always be there in your time of need, whether it be to celebrate your successes or mourn your losses; someone who you genuinely wanted to spend time with. That was Brielle.

As badly as I wanted to blow off Kentucky and spend a quiet Christmas at home with her, my mother had been abundantly clear that full family attendance for Christmas was non-negotiable. I'd missed the last few years because I'd had to work. Being the low man on the totem pole, it was an unwritten rule that you stepped up to cover for the more senior guys to work holidays, but I'd managed to get this year off.

"Come to Kentucky with me."

"What?"

"Come with me."

She bit her lip. "I don't know if I should."

"I promise it won't be as intense as the party. My parents won't be trying to impress. It'll only be family." That reminded me. "Plus, you sort of already told Mother that you'd come, so she's counting on that."

She tilted her head back onto the seat. "I did, didn't I?"

"Yup."

She sighed. "If I do this, then you have to do something for me."

"Anything."

"I'm having dinner with my parents on Friday night to celebrate early since they won't be in town. Come with me."

I grinned and snuck a glance at her. "I'd love to." It felt like a very boyfriend thing to do and I liked the sound of that. Even if her father wasn't my biggest fan.

Brielle squeezed my arm. "Then I guess I'm going to Kentucky."

I desperately wanted to kiss her.

THE SUN HAD ALREADY SET when I pulled up to our building and I put it in park by the valet. It took a few minutes to get the tree down from the roof, but once I did, I carried it carefully through the doorway and Brielle helped me load it into the elevator. I'd gone earlier that day to buy a tree stand and I'd already put it in place by one of the floor-to-ceiling windows in the living room. While I held the tree in place, Brielle screwed it into the stand. We stepped back to admire it. It truly was perfect.

"Now we decorate," I said as I grabbed the shopping bags of stuff I'd purchased that morning.

"First things first." Brielle pulled out her phone and turned on holiday music, streaming it through the Bluetooth house speakers. Then she crossed to the kitchen. "We also need wine." She poured us glasses of Cabernet while I unboxed the white string lights. She held the glass out to me. "Cheers."

"To our first Christmas," I said, making us both smile as we clinked our glasses, then took sips. I put my wine down on the coffee table.

"One more thing." Brielle got up on her toes and kissed me softly on the lips. "Now we can decorate."

We wrapped the lights around the tree then scattered the various blue and white ornaments throughout the branches. We stopped long enough to belt out Mariah Carey's "All I Want for Christmas." Well, Brielle did most of the singing. I mostly hummed along while we bounced around the room. It was best that way, trust me.

We looped the silver garland over the branches, then I handed Brielle the star and picked her up so she could place it on top. Once in place, we stepped back to admire our work.

"It's perfect," she uttered.

"Almost." I pulled a small gift bag out from amongst the empty boxes. When she wasn't looking, I'd slipped the ornament from the tree farm into it with my other surprise. I handed her the bag.

"What's this?" she asked, taking it.

"Open it."

"But Christmas isn't for another ten days."

"Just open it," I urged.

She pulled out the tissue paper and dug her hand into the small bag, pulling out the porcelain Christmas tree with the name of the farm we'd gone to and the year printed on the bottom. She grinned. "When did you do this?"

"Magic. There's something else still in there."

She retrieved the hand-blown glass Rockette ornament that I'd bought from Radio City Music Hall before I'd picked her up from work earlier that day.

Her jaw dropped. "Keith," she trailed off as she stared at the figure.

"Do you like it?"

"Like it? No. I absolutely love it." Her smile made my chest clench. "Thank you. These are exactly what we needed." She turned to the tree and took great care finding prominent spots for both of them, then she stepped back and sighed. "Now it's perfect."

I came up behind her and wrapped her in my arms, inhaling the sweet scent of peonies and the pine that had infiltrated her skin. She leaned into me. Holding her felt right—as though our bodies had been created for each other like puzzle pieces. I could only imagine how perfect she'd feel when I was inside of her.

"Keith?"

"Yeah, Elle?"

"I could get used to this."

"That makes two of us."

She spun around in my embrace and laced her fingers behind my neck. "You know, I seem to remember we were in the middle of something the other night that got interrupted." Her voice dipped low and spoke directly to my groin.

"Oh, do you?"

"I do." She rose up onto her toes, bringing her mouth close to mine. "It's kind of all I've been able to think about these past few days." She licked her lip and I salivated with the desire to taste her.

"Yeah?" I whispered.

"Yeah," she whispered back.

I brought my mouth within millimeters of hers and said, "I think we should do something about that then."

Her lips grazed mine as she replied, "Me, too."

The tip of my tongue darted out and skimmed over the

crease of her mouth. Her lips parted, making way for mine, and I took the opportunity to take our teasing deeper into a kiss. She pressed her tits against my chest and I tightened my hold on her back, bringing her even closer. She moaned as my tongue found hers and her hands worked their way up into my hair.

She tasted like the best decision I'd ever made. My hands dropped to her ass and once my palms were full of her I squeezed and tilted my pelvis forward. My dick was straining in my jeans—craving her. My desire for Brielle was beyond *want*. I'd even passed *had to have* and was firmly sitting in *need*. I needed to know what I'd been missing all of those years. I needed to see how deep our friendship ran.

She tugged at the hem of my t-shirt and I happily obliged her by lifting it over my head, only breaking our kiss for the briefest moment. Her fingernails scraped down my chest and over my abs, then back up again and over my shoulders, sending chills down my back. I had to feel her skin against mine, so I gripped the bottom of her sweater and jerked it off of her. I'd planned to go right back into a kiss, but the sight of her on display for me caused me to pause to admire her. She wore a simple white satin bra and I swear on my life I'd never seen anything sexier. The bright white was divine against her latte-colored skin and the way it shaped her full, luscious, tits was mesmerizing.

Like a magnet, they pulled me in. I took handfuls of her as I dove my face into her cleavage, massaging her as I nipped at the curve of her exposed skin. Her head dipped back and she released a deep-toned breath. I licked a trail up from between her tits, over to her collarbone, then up her neck to her ear. After pulling her ear lobe into my mouth, I bit down hard enough to make her jolt. My hand skirted up to her throat and I gripped it as I clenched the lobe between my teeth. She gasped and I pushed her backward with my body until we were at the couch, then I laid her down and lowered myself on top of her, claiming her mouth again.

She gyrated beneath me and I answered each rise of her pelvis with a thrust of my hips, making her feel what she was doing to me—how hard she was making me. My palm went for her chest, cupping her, and she pulled her mouth from mine before diving into the crook of my neck. I had a particularly sensitive spot where my trap muscle met my collarbone and her lips found it like she somehow knew it was there.

I cried out, "Oh, Fuck."

She sucked, making me shiver.

"Yes," I begged for more as ripples of pleasure exploded inside me like shockwaves.

She bit down and I was nearly a goner. I ground my throbbing cock against her as though I could fuck her through our jeans. Her mouth suctioned to me and I grunted through my teeth. She released me and I almost collapsed on top of her, panting.

Her thumbs hooked into my waistband. "I can feel how hard you are, but I want more."

Fuck, so did I. I worked to catch my breath. "Elle." Saying her name—my name for her—zapped me back to reality. Having sex would be our point of no return. My willpower had been shot full of holes, but I still managed to whisper, "Are you sure?"

"Yes." The word was out of her mouth as though it had been a part of my same breath.

I pushed up, hovering over her, so I could look her in the eyes. They were dark and wanting and I lavished in being the recipient of what I was sure was the sexiest dang *fuck me* stare Brielle has ever given.

"We can't undo this if we..."

She reached up and brushed an unruly wave of hair off my forehead. "I know."

I bit my lip as I warred with myself over what to do: listen to my mind or listen to my body.

Brielle ran her thumb over my bottom lip making me release it from my teeth. "Keith, this has been years in the making. Stop being a gentleman and give me what I need."

What was left of my willpower crumbled. Hell, I needed it, too.

I forced myself to get off of her and grabbed her by the hands, pulling her up with me, then I led her to my bedroom. Before I could get us onto the bed, she wrapped her arms around me from behind and expertly unfastened the button on my jeans, then carefully tugged down the zipper. Her hand dove into my pants and cupped my cock through my boxer briefs.

She moaned with appreciation. "Damn."

I reached around and grabbed her, dislodging her hand and pushing her down onto my bed. After dropping my pants, I went for the button on her jeans. She lifted her hips, allowing me to free her legs from the denim. With my hands resting atop her thighs, I admired her fit body in the white satin thong that matched her bra. I gripped her hips and tossed her further onto the bed so I could get on top.

While I went in for another kiss, her hands slipped between us and she clutched my swollen cock through the thin layer of cotton that still separated us. As badly as I needed her, I wanted to take my time. Admittedly, there was also a part of me that wanted to go slow enough to give us a chance to change our minds before it was absolutely too late. Once I was inside of her, she would be mine, and I needed to be sure, beyond a shadow of a doubt, that she wanted that, too, because there'd be no way in hell I could go back to simply being her friend after I claimed her.

My tongue caressed hers and I leaned into her palm, making her feel the weight of my erection. Her narrow fingers wrapped around me and I was ready to break through my underwear.

"Off," she murmured into my mouth.

I hesitated.

She felt it.

I tried to keep kissing her, but she turned her head, making me pull away and look at her. She released my cock and rubbed her hands up my back. "If you're not ready, it's okay." The tenderness in her gaze threatened to unravel me.

"It's not that. I want this, trust me. I *need* this."

"Then what is it?"

I took a deep breath. "I just...want to be sure..."

"If it makes you feel any better, I've never been surer of anything—anyone—in my life. You mean the world to me Keith and I wouldn't jeopardize that." She'd said everything I needed to hear. She'd put words to the feelings that had been dancing around in my head that entire night.

I rested my forehead on hers. "I promise to take care of you. And, no matter what, you'll always be my Elle."

She cradled my face in her hands. "Always." Her head tilted back and she pressed her lips between my brows. "Show me how good we can be, Keith."

I kissed the dip in her throat and worked my lips down her chest. My hand slipped behind Brielle's back and I glanced up at her as I unsnapped her bra. She wasted no time discarding it, putting herself on display for me. I'd fantasized about those tits and they were even more spectacular in real-life. They were full and crested with her chocolate kiss nipples.

I palmed her and they overflowed my hands. My breath

heaved as I massaged her bare flesh. Then my tongue sought out and flicked against one of her peaks, causing her back to arch, thrusting more of her into my mouth and I sucked her in.

She gripped the bed sheet in her fists and gasped as my thumb brushed against her other nipple before switching to take it into my mouth. I liked how sensitive she was and I imagined I'd be spending a lot of time testing that sensitivity. Wondering where else she was sensitive, my hand crept between our bodies and found the cool satin of her thong. I dipped a little lower and was met with heat and a slickness that told me she was ready for me.

Her panties needed to go. I propped up to my knees and lifted her legs straight up so that they rested against my shoulder. I hooked my fingers into the narrow elastic over the sides of her hips and she lifted her ass off of the bed for me. While I slowly dragged her panties from her legs, my eyes met hers and they were filled with a fire that I felt deep inside. After depositing the white satin on the floor, I wrapped my fingers around her ankles and broke our eye contact as I spread her legs apart, opening her up to me completely.

I bit my lip and moaned with approval. "You've got a gorgeous pussy." She was neatly trimmed and the short dark hairs pointed to her swollen pink clit. My mouth watered. I dropped her ankles and her legs fell to the sides as I scooted down so I could taste her. Taking my time, I trailed kisses up one thigh, then lightly blew air over her center, making her squirm, before kissing down her other thigh. I did it again, this time stopping to nibble on the crease of her pubic bone.

"Keith, please," she begged as she bucked her hips.

"Tell me what you want."

"I want..." She panted. "You to..."

"What do you want me to do to you?"

She whimpered.

So, she was shy. Got it. I coaxed her, "Do you want me to make you feel good?"

"Yes," she breathed.

"How?" I kissed her mound just above her bud, making her cry out. "Do you want me to put my mouth on your pretty pussy?"

"Yes. Please."

I nibbled on the spot just above her clit, letting my chin rest against the bundle of nerves. "Do you want to come on my tongue, Elle?"

She bucked wildly with need. "Yes," she exulted.

I made the contact she'd been craving and fuck she let out this deep moan of pleasure that made me feel invincible. I lapped at her, tasting her sweet nectar as it lathered my chin. It took hardly any time at all for her orgasm to build. Her whole body tensed and just before she was about to release, I could feel her lifting away from me, so I held on and forced her to ride out her pleasure on my tongue. She screamed and her thighs shook around my head while she rode my mouth to ecstasy.

It was by far the most incredible thing I'd ever seen. "Shit, Elle," I muttered as she came down from her high. Her whole dang body shook.

"I need...you...inside me...now," she declared between breaths.

After what I'd just witnessed, she didn't have to tell me twice. I stood up and lost my boxer briefs, letting my stiff cock spring free. I jerked it a few times as I dug through my night-stand for a condom. Upon finding one, I wasted no time tearing through the foil and rolling it on.

I positioned myself on top of her, in awe of how her chest still heaved and the burning desire written all over her face. Gripping my shaft, I ran it up and down her slit a few times to coat it in her juices. I needed her something fierce.

Leaning forward, I gave her a kiss, then asked, "You ready?"

She nodded and her arms flailed beside me. "Yes. Give it to me."

I pushed back to my knees because I needed to see myself enter her for the first time. I lined my head up with her bright pink opening and took a couple of steadying breaths. I'd never been so nervous to have sex before. This meant something. She meant something. More than anyone else ever had.

I eased forward feeling her walls open up around my head. She was still tense from her orgasm, so it took a few pushes to get more than the tip in, but once I had, she stretched around me until I was fully seated inside of her.

Point of no return.

We moaned in unison as another piece of the puzzle clicked into place.

She was tight as fuck and so dang wet, it dripped down my balls and I hadn't even moved yet. I think I was in shock. I was inside Brielle Jackson. *My Elle. Holy shit.*

She gripped behind her knees and pulled her legs to her stomach. "More." The pleading in her voice snapped me out of it and I began to rock inside of her.

I leaned toward her and she put her ankles on my shoulders, bending in half, as I continued to stretch her with each thrust in and out.

"Yes. Yes, yes, yes. Yes," she chanted and I felt her body tense up again.

Gradually increasing my pace, I surged forward, letting my balls smack her in the ass. Her legs began to shake and her breathing quickened. I reached between us and pressed down hard on her clit with my thumb. Without having to move it to stimulate her, she exploded on my cock, gripping me tightly inside of her, as her body convulsed and her eyes rolled to the back of her head. I kept her pinned down with my torso as I moved faster.

She panted like she'd just run a dang marathon. "Keith." My name hung on her tongue like it was the secret password to her deepest desires.

Reaching up, I pinched her nipples, causing her to arch upward. *Yes, I was going to have fun with those.* Her legs slipped down and I moved my arms so she could drop them to the bed, but instead she hooked her ankles behind my ass and held me deep inside of her. So deep.

I kept still and kissed her. She devoured me like I was her first meal after a period of starvation. My balls clenched as her tongue traced along my top lip. She released my mouth to go for my neck, and she found that sensitive spot at the crux of my collarbone and my trap muscle again.

I inhaled sharply as my cock jerked between her walls. Forcing myself to focus, I began to move again, keeping pace with the urgency of her mouth on my neck. It didn't take long for the pressure to build up in my shaft.

She sucked hard on my spot and I buried myself in her pussy just as my release reached the tip, and I unloaded inside of her with a growl. My heart raced and the world went black for a moment while I rode the wave. It'd been a long time since I'd come that hard. *If* I'd ever come that hard before at all. I held still as I twitched within her walls and she ran her hands through my sweat-laden hair.

When I finally opened my lids and stared into her dark eyes, she smiled up at me and it dang near took away what was left of my breath.

"Elle," I whispered.

"Keith," she returned in just as hushed a tone.

No other words were needed. Without a doubt, *this* was

where we belonged. And I had every intention of keeping her. Forever.

TEN

BRIELLE

I stood in my bathroom wearing a garnet-red lace bra and thong that perfectly matched the dress I planned on wearing to dinner with my parents that evening, while using the hot curling iron to refresh my curls. One good thing about my job was that I had professional hair and makeup services every day, so whenever I was going out, all I had to do was get dressed. It had been snowing that afternoon, though, so my hair had gotten wet and my curls needed a little refresher before Keith and I went to dinner with my parents.

After Wednesday night, I hadn't been able to stop thinking about him and how he'd felt inside of me. If I closed my eyes, I could practically still feel him there. We hadn't had a chance to do it again because he had worked Thursday night, so I was buzzing with need. When I'd gotten home from work that afternoon, Keith had been sleeping. He'd texted me when he'd gotten home that morning to say that he'd had a long night, so he was going to nap before dinner.

As badly as I'd wanted to curl up in bed with him, I hadn't had the heart to wake him, but I was already looking forward to getting home after dinner and having a repeat of Wednesday night. I hummed along to the acoustic Christmas music that played softly on my phone while I wrapped the last strand of my hair around the curling iron.

After thoroughly checking in the mirror to make sure I hadn't missed a spot, I turned to go back to my room and nearly jumped out of my skin when I saw Keith leaning against the doorframe, watching me. Shirtless.

He had his lip between his teeth and his copper eyes took their time soaking in every inch of me. "Do you have any idea how fucking sexy you are?" His voice was deep and filled with need.

I grinned as I admired his carved abs and his broad chest and his chiseled biceps. "Do you have any idea how fucking sexy you are?" I echoed.

He stepped into the bathroom and reached for me, gripping my hips in his strong hands. "How much time until we have to leave for dinner?"

My lady parts tingled and I seriously considered skipping dinner all together. I glanced at the time on my phone. "Twenty minutes." Judging by his bed head, I guessed he still needed to shower and what I wanted to do to him would take longer than twenty minutes.

"You sure?" he grumbled, as his hands traveled up my sides.

I nodded. "I'm sure."

He pouted. "Maybe we can be a little late?"

"Maybe I give you a little something to hold you over until later?" I reached for the growing bulge in his sweatpants.

He sucked in a sharp breath.

I rolled onto my tip-toes and kissed him, taking us deep from the start. Keith's hands migrated over to my bra and he squeezed my breasts through the lace. I pulled away from our kiss and dropped to my knees, never letting my eyes leave his.

The copper was swallowed up by his pupils when he realized what my plan was. I reached into his waistband and freed his erection, which was nearly at full mast. Keith was big, but not intimidatingly so. He was perfect, really.

He smelled musky and manly and the bead of pre-cum on his tip begged for my tongue. I hadn't gotten to taste him the other night because after the full-body orgasm he'd given me, I'd been desperate to feel him. I parted my lips and kept my eyes locked to his as I allowed the tip of my tongue to trace his opening. He inhaled sharply and jerked in my hand.

I stroked him a couple of times while I softly kissed his head before taking it into my mouth so I could run my tongue along the ridge where his dome met his shaft. As desperately as I wanted to take all of him, that wasn't the plan. I sucked in my cheeks, creating a vacuum effect as I popped him out of my mouth, making him moan.

"Oh, shit, Elle." His mouth hung open.

I released him and stood up. Placing my palm flat on his chest, I leaned toward his ear and whispered, "To be continued."

He whimpered. "You're killing me."

I smirked. "Something to look forward to." As I went to step around him, he slapped my ass, sending an unexpected jolt of pleasure to my core. I hummed. "Later." Out the door I went.

NINETEEN MINUTES LATER, we were in Keith's Range Rover on our way to Long Island. Growing up, when we weren't living in London, we lived in my grandparents' house in Roslyn, which worked well since my parents sometimes had to leave me there while they traveled. When Nan and Pop had passed away while I was in high school, they'd left the house to my parents and my father lived there full-time, whereas my mother split her time between New York and their flat in London.

Friday night traffic was miserable during the holidays. Especially so on a day when it had snowed enough to make the roads wet and the cold threatened to ice them over. We finally made it through the tunnel to the Long Island Expressway. Despite the fact that we'd accounted for traffic when planning what time we had to leave, we were running late. I'd texted my parents to let them know so they could try and change our reservation.

"Out of curiosity," Keith asked, "What exactly did you tell your parents when you said I was coming with you?" He was fishing.

I wasn't falling for it. "That I wanted to bring you."

Through the corner of my eye, I observed him rubbing his lips together, no doubt trying to come up with another way to phrase what he was asking.

I let him off the hook, but I also turned it back on him. "Are you asking if I told them that my roommate was coming or... something else?"

"Something else?" He flipped it to me.

"What did you want me to tell them?"

He merged into the restricted HOV lane. Hopefully that would get us through the traffic quicker. He sighed. "I want to be your something else, Elle."

I grinned. "Then I guess it's a good thing that I told them I wanted to bring my boyfriend."

He took his eyes off the road for a moment and stared at me brightly. "Really?"

I nodded. "Really." Perhaps it had been presumptuous of me, but judging by the smile on Keith's face, it seemed I had presumed correctly. Still, I asked, "That okay with you?"

"Baby, that is more than okay."

My heart surged. *He called me baby.*

"Does your father know that it's me you're dating?"

I'd left that part out when I'd spoken to my parents. Let's just say that my dad wasn't thrilled that I had a roommate of the opposite sex. When I'd first moved in with Keith, Dad had insisted on meeting him. It hadn't exactly gone well. My dad had spent the entire time accusing Keith of trying to get into my pants.

This dinner should be fun...

"Not exactly," I replied.

"Elle, he's going to kill me."

"No, he won't. He didn't give you a chance last time. I'm sure once he actually gets to know you, he'll adore you like I do."

We pulled up to the Clocktower Grille which was my favorite restaurant in Roslyn. It was down the road from the iconic granite and sandstone Clock Tower and sat on Roslyn Pond Park, which was lit up with lights for Christmas. My parents weren't big on driving at night, so I was happy to make the trip back to my hometown. We valeted the car and I took Keith's arm as we made our way inside. The hostess checked our coats and I took a moment to admire how sexy Keith looked in his hunter-green sweater and gray dress pants. We'd been rushing to leave the apartment, so I hadn't had a chance to get a real good look at him before. Keith was always nice to look at, but when he got dressed up, my ovaries felt it.

The restaurant was normally bright and airy, but for the holidays they'd managed to cozy it up with decorations— pinecones, wreaths, red bows—and darker linens. The woman showed us to our table by the window where my parents were already seated. Mom saw me first and she nudged my dad to stand. I released Keith and went straight for her. It'd been three months since I'd seen my mom.

"Mom that dress is stunning on you." It was a classic black wool halter dress

"Thanks. It's vintage Chanel." Not only had I inherited my mother's features, but I also got her love for fashion. Coco Chanel had created the Little Black Dress, so it was no wonder that the dress was divine.

Keith hung back and waited for me to hug them both, and then I stepped to the side to introduce him.

"Mom, Dad. This is my boyfriend, Keith Hart." Saying it out loud made me giddy.

My father's smile drooped.

Mom pulled Keith in for a hug. "It's wonderful to meet you, Keith. We were so glad to hear that you'd be joining us."

Perhaps I should mention that I hadn't introduced my parents to a boyfriend in four years. Not since Mitchell.

Keith held his hand out to my dad. "Pleasure to see you again, sir."

Dad stood there with his hands in the pockets of his tweed jacket while his eyes surveyed Keith. I thought Dad was actually going to leave him hanging for a sec, but then he begrudgingly took Keith's hand and said in his deep, broadcasting voice, "So much for just friends, I see."

"Dad!"

"Douglas!"

Mom and I scolded him as he returned to his seat. Keith held my chair out for me and waited until us ladies were seated before sitting himself.

He took my dad's dig on the chin. "I'd like to be clear upfront that dating your daughter was never my intention when we'd moved in together. We've been close friends for years and neither one of us took it lightly when we decided to enter into this relationship. I can assure you that I would never jeopardize our friendship if I didn't believe that being with her was worth it." Spoken like the son of a politician and a debutante. Keith amazed me. He had two sides to him: The old-world southern gentleman and the crass FDNY fireman. I adored them both and I was grateful he allowed me to see all parts of him.

My mother responded first. "That is lovely to hear, Keith. Thank you for your honesty." She turned to my father. "Right, Douglas?"

My father's dark eyes loomed over his glasses and bore into Keith. "I suppose."

I was not going to let that set the tone for the night. "Dad, stop it. Regardless of whether Keith and I are dating or not, he's one of my best friends, so play nice."

He dipped his chin. "All right." Then he reached for his scotch and water and took a sip. It was the only alcohol he drank, and he mostly reserved it for special occasions.

I turned my attention to Mom. "How was Prague?" Her latest assignment had her there covering the Czech Republic's potential adoption of the euro, which was something they'd committed to in 2004 when they joined the EU, but had never executed.

Mom relayed the details from her recent trip. Her accent hovered between being American and British, depending on the word. She was interrupted when our waiter came over to tell us the specials and take Keith's and my drink orders.

I turned to Keith. "Choose a wine for me?" Since living with him I'd learned that he had impeccable taste in wine.

His lips turned up and he said, "The lady and I will both have a glass of your Tempranillo."

Mom seemed impressed. "You're a fan of Spanish wines?"

Keith nodded. "My parents are connoisseurs. I'd tried more varieties of wine by my eighteenth birthday than I had sodas."

"What do your parents do, Keith?" my father asked.

I unconsciously held my breath, since Keith didn't like to talk about his parents, and waited to see how he'd respond.

He didn't miss a beat. "My mother is on the board for several charitable organizations and my father is in politics."

Mom snuck a glance at me and Dad pursed his lips. I was certain they were thinking about Mitchell. I placed a hand on Keith's thigh.

Dad continued, "Politics, huh? Whereabouts?"

To Keith's credit, he was transparent even though I knew he didn't want to be. "He's one of the senators from Kentucky."

Both of my parents' eyes widened. Rightfully so. It was a big deal. Mom replied, "That's quite impressive."

Keith nodded. "He's been in politics ever since he got out of the Army when I was a kid."

My father tapped on the table. "Are you referring to Senator Graham Hart? The Colonel and former governor?"

I was impressed that my father had heard of Keith's dad, given his history as a foreign correspondent, although I couldn't say I was all that surprised since as a professor here in the States, he was more well-versed on national news than previously.

"Yes, sir," Keith replied.

I watched my father soften. "He performs quite favorably in the polls."

Keith nodded. "He's very good at his job. My brother's following in his footsteps."

"And you're a fireman."

Keith tensed.

"That's a very noble profession," Mom contributed.

"Thank you, ma'am."

She waved Keith off. "None of this ma'am business. Please, call me Kim."

Dad added, "Has that been difficult for you?" As journalists, nothing got by my parents and they were never afraid to ask the hard questions that most people shied away from—socially acceptable or not.

Keith ran his tongue along his teeth. "Not being in the family business, you mean?"

"Yes," my father replied.

Keith sighed. "My parents would prefer it if I were."

Mom offered a thoughtful smile and I expected her to say something, but my father surprised me by commenting, "That's a shame. As my wife said, what you do is very noble. You should be proud."

Some of Keith's tension eased. "Thank you, sir."

Dad nodded. "Kim and I hadn't expected Brielle to go into journalism like we did, but she's got a real knack for it. We would've encouraged her to do anything she wanted to—journalism or not."

The waiter returned with our wine and I immediately reached for mine as we ordered our meals.

Once the waiter had left, my father swirled the ice in his rocks glass. "I feel for you, son. My father was a mechanic and he believed that real men worked with their hands." He took a sip of his scotch. "You should've seen the disappointment on his face when I told him that I wanted to go to college instead of take over his auto body shop."

I'd never known that. Pops had always seemed content with my dad's career choice.

Keith nodded. "I can certainly relate. Being a fireman was my dream, though, and I wasn't willing to give it up. I'm still not." He tapped the side of his wine glass. "Did your father ever come to understand your decision?" He was genuinely asking my dad for advice and it melted my heart.

Dad smirked. "It took time." He wrapped his arm around my mom. After thirty-one years together, they were still hopelessly in love. "But when I met this incredible woman overseas on assignment, my father's heart softened for her just like mine had. And when Brielle was born, it became water under the bridge. He saw how happy my choice had made me and he learned to respect it."

Keith brought his wine glass to his lips. "That's good to hear." He took a sip and then changed the subject. "Has Brielle told you about her talks with Senator Patten?"

My parents' ears perked up and Mom asked, "What kind of talks?"

I spent the next fifteen minutes gushing about my passion project. Dinner was on the table by the time I'd gotten into explaining the task force we were assembling.

My parents couldn't contain their pride. Dad said, "You never cease to amaze me, bunny." He'd called me that since I was a little girl. He then addressed Keith. "Thank you for helping her have that opportunity."

I had told them that I'd met the senator at Keith's parents' party.

Keith shook his head. "I had nothing to do with it. That was all her. I simply got her in the door."

Dad beamed. "Everything our daughter has achieved she's worked hard for. Not once has she asked us to make a call for her, even though we would in a heartbeat."

Dinner had been cleared and Keith's arm rested on the back of my chair. He looked at me with a sparkle in his eyes. "For as long as I've known her, Brielle has never been afraid of going after what she wants." He winked.

I blushed. While we'd both had a hand in us getting together, I suppose I was the one who'd tipped the scale. And I was so grateful that I had.

As our evening came to an end, we walked toward the front

together and waited in the entrance for the valet to bring our cars. I hugged my parents and wished them a safe trip.

Mom wrapped her arms around Keith. "It was lovely spending this time together. We must do it again the next time I'm in town."

"Absolutely."

Dad surprised us all when he extended his hand to Keith and then pulled him in for a quick hug as well. "Once I get back from London next month, perhaps you can give me a tour of your firehouse. I'd love to see it."

My heart fluttered and I couldn't have loved my dad more than I did in that moment. He was a perceptive man and I wondered if he knew just how much his offer would mean to Keith.

Keith's smile couldn't have gotten any bigger. "I'd be happy to show you around, sir."

"Please, call me Douglas."

Keith gave him a hard nod. "Douglas."

I'D FALLEN asleep on the ride home, which only took about thirty minutes as opposed to the hour and fifteen it had taken us to get there. Cars tended to do that to me. Especially at night. One thing about my job, it made me a grandma when it came to staying up late.

Keith caressed my shoulder. "We're home."

The doorman opened my door for me and I sleepily hopped out and leaned on Keith as we made our way upstairs. I kicked off my shoes and plopped down on the couch, then patted the space beside me, which Keith happily filled.

I leaned my head on his shoulder. "Thank you for coming with me tonight."

He kissed the top of my head. "Thank you for inviting me. I really enjoyed it."

"I told you my dad would come around."

He laughed. "Yes, you did. I'm glad. It was really nice." He sighed. "I can't remember ever having a family meal like that with my parents. Everything is always a production and inevitably ends with me getting pissed off about their disapproval."

I stretched my arm around to hug him. "You should never have to try so hard to impress someone. Who you are is more than enough. Remember that."

"Wise words."

I nodded. "My dad taught me that. He's been saying it since I was little."

"You're lucky, Elle."

I tilted my chin up and kissed his jaw. "As long as you have me, you'll have them."

He turned his head down to look at me and teased, "I guess we'd better make this work then, huh?"

I cupped his cheek. "I recall making you a promise earlier."

He bit his lower lip. "Yes, you did."

"I assume you want to collect on that promise." I was aching to feel him inside of me again.

"Hell, yes." He kissed me and I realized exactly how lucky I truly was.

ELEVEN

KEITH

The day before Christmas Eve, our flight landed in Louisville, Kentucky and we hopped into the car my parents had booked to collect us and drive us the fifty minutes to Frankfort. I hadn't been back to my hometown since college. I usually saw my parents in D.C. since it was an easy four-hour drive from New York and my father spent most of his time there anyway.

Brielle was well-traveled when it came to international trips, but she'd never been to the true American south. This would be interesting. We pulled into town, the water tower standing prominently to mark our arrival. The reality of how different my life had become was apparent as we drove through downtown. The railroad ran through the center and most of the buildings were quaint and historic. Being the Bourbon capital, there was no shortage of bars and distilleries. Being the state capital, there were several government buildings and the entire town was decorated for Christmas.

White lights wrapped around the lamp posts and several of the historic buildings had up wreaths and bows. We passed the

Governor's Mansion and I pointed it out to Brielle. "That's where I lived for eight years."

Her jaw dropped. "Wow. It's beautiful."

I nodded. "It was modeled after Queen Marie Antoinette's villa on the grounds of the Palace of Versailles and it's built from stone mined here in Kentucky."

Her eyes widened. "So you basically grew up in a palace?"

I laughed. "Maybe we can go check it out later."

"I'd love that."

My family's home was another ten minutes past downtown in farm country. When my father had graduated from Governor to Senator, my parents had purchased a one-million-dollar, six-thousand square foot home on eight acres. It was overkill. But it also put things into perspective in comparison to what double that money got them in D.C.

Our driveway was just under half a mile long. When we pulled up, it became apparent that my parents hadn't spared a cent when it came to Christmas decorations. There was a tree in front that rivaled the one at the New Capitol Building and lights bordered the entire house.

Brielle's jaw hung slack. "This is your house?"

Feeling a little self-conscious, I replied, "I've only lived here for maybe nine months of my life."

Undeniably, the home was magnificent. It had a pool, sauna, full gym, a game room, a movie theater complete with projector screen and eight recliners, as well as the requisite wine cellar. There was also a stable for horses, but my mother had given them up a couple of years ago. D.C. was their primary home and they only spent about two months in total in Kentucky, so it made no sense to keep the horses. Besides, she never rode them. I swear she only kept them because it was the *proper* thing to do in the south.

The car parked right in front to let us out. Brielle went to the trunk to get her bag, but I shook my head. "Geoffrey will take care of them."

"He's here?"

I nodded. "Arina stays in D.C., but Geoffrey travels with my parents. There's more staff here, as well that you'll meet."

Her eyes widened, but before she could say anything, my mother appeared on the porch. "Welcome home, darling."

I grasped Brielle's hand in mine and we made our way up the steps. "Hello, Mother." I greeted her with a kiss by each cheek and then Brielle did the same.

"I am so pleased you have both made it. How was the flight?"

"Fine," I replied. We went inside to escape the cold. It was about fifteen degrees warmer than New York, but there was still a chill in the air.

Once inside, Geoffrey greeted us and took our coats, then we went to the parlor, which was decorated in similar fashion to the reception room at the Governor's Mansion. It had an old world feel to it and was packed with antiques I was afraid to add up the value of. There was also an impeccably decorated Christmas tree and three knit stockings hung on the mantle, clearly for show. We sat on one of the fancy sofas while my mother instructed Geoffrey to gather the others, then she took her spot in one of the armchairs by the fireplace.

"I am delighted you both could make it. It has been too long since you have been home for Christmas, darling." She knew how to lay on the guilt.

"As I've explained, Mother, I've worked the last few years so that the guys in my firehouse with kids could be off."

She hummed. "Brielle, sugar, when do you think you and Keith will decide to have kids."

I about choked on my saliva. "Mother!"

"What?" she feigned stupid. "It is a perfectly reasonable

question. Brielle is working hard on her career right now, so I understand if she is not ready, yet, but I would like to know when she anticipates being ready."

I was ready for a drink, even if it was only two in the afternoon. "I'm not there yet either, Mother. I'd like to at least make lieutenant first before—"

"Yes, yes. Brielle, what do you think? A year? Two?"

Corbett and Caroline entered, saving us from my mother's inquisition. They'd arrived two days earlier. After we greeted them, they took seats on the opposite sofa.

"Where's the Colonel?" I asked.

Mother exaggerated a sigh. "He had to go into the office for something. I mean really, what is so important that it cannot wait a couple of days? Tomorrow is Christmas Eve for heaven's sake."

And there was my out. "I promised Brielle I'd give her a tour of Frankfort. Perhaps we should go now while the Colonel is in the Capitol, so he can show us around."

"What a wonderful idea, darling. I am sure your father would be elated to see you."

Ten minutes later, I'd managed to successfully extricate us from my mother's grasp. I borrowed one of the cars on the property and drove us toward downtown. "I'm sorry. I don't know why I thought coming down here would be a good idea."

Brielle placed her hand on mine. "No apologizing, I knew what I was getting into when I agreed to four days with your family."

I hated that that was a thing and desperately wished there was some kind of normalcy when it came to my family. Our first stop was the New Capitol where my father had an office. I figured if we went there first, we could get it out of the way and then do our own thing. We passed the large Christmas tree out front as I navigated us to the parking lot.

Once inside I called my father and he came to meet us a few minutes later.

"Brielle, how wonderful to see you again." He hugged my girlfriend before shaking my hand. "Come, I'll show you around." He gave us an abbreviated tour of the building, pointing out the French inspired architecture and the valuable artwork on the walls.

"Have you taken Brielle to the Governor's Mansion?" he asked.

"That's next," I replied.

"Splendid. I'll call over there and prepare them for your arrival."

"Thanks, Colonel."

He brought us up to his office. "Brielle, I was hoping your parents would have come with."

I huffed. "As I explained to Mother, Brielle's parents are in London."

"Yes, yes. Of course. I do hope we have the pleasure of meeting them soon."

Brielle snuck a glance at me and I tried to apologize for my father's behavior with my eyes. She replied, "Perhaps we can arrange something once they're home."

"Outstanding," my father replied.

"Thanks for showing us around, Colonel, but we must be going. There are several places I'd like to take Brielle before they close."

We said our goodbyes and got back in the car.

"I'm sorry about him. I'm not sure what his motive is behind meeting your parents."

She waved me off. "Not to worry."

I drove us the few blocks to the Mansion, then parked the car. I held Brielle's hand while we walked through the front garden. In my opinion, there was no prettier place at Christmas than the Mansion. The stone balustrade on the front portico was draped with natural garland and white lights while live wreaths with red bows hung between the four sets of stone pillars that spanned the full two-stories. The decorations were in no short supply. I hadn't been back there in years and it was interesting because being at the Governor's Mansion felt more like I was coming home than my parents' place did.

The Mansion was known as The People's House because it was open to the public, so I let myself in and was greeted almost immediately by Elek, who had been the houseman there for nearly thirty years. He was originally from Hungary and still had his accent, which I remembered as being a nice reprieve from the southern drawl of the other staffers.

"Keith Hart," he exclaimed as he made his way toward us and zealously shook my hands. "Talk about a Christmas miracle."

I laughed. "It's great to see you, Elek. It has been too long." I motioned toward Brielle. "This is my girlfriend, Brielle Jackson. I wanted to show her where I grew up if you don't mind."

He puffed out air. "Of course not. You know your way. The first family is away from the residence for the holiday, so feel free to roam about."

"Thank you, Elek."

As we milled about, I showed off all of the rooms filled with antiques and artwork, but most importantly, it was decorated to the gills for Christmas. The whole place smelled of pine and cinnamon and each room was adorned with twinkling lights, natural garland, and plenty of red and gold everything.

"Now I understand why you insisted on chopping down our own tree," she commented as we checked out the seventh live tree in the Mansion.

"Why's that?"

"Because this is all magnificent. If this is what you're used to, then I'm surprised our living room doesn't look like a window display at Saks 5ᵗʰ Avenue."

I laughed. "It's amazing, isn't it?"

"Absolutely."

I pulled her in for a hug. I'd never brought a girl back to the Mansion with me before and it felt incredibly right holding her there in the Family Dining Room. I almost wanted to smack myself for not seeing it sooner. Brielle and I belonged together.

We made our way to the kitchen where I found Brady, the head chef.

"Keith Hart? Is it really you?" He put down his knife and wiped his hands on his apron.

"Hey Brady. How've you been?"

He gave me a quick hug and I introduced him to Brielle.

"I wish I knew you were coming; I would've made you something special."

"I appreciate the thought, Brady."

"What have you been up to?" he asked.

"I'm a firefighter in New York City."

His brows raised. "No kidding. That is super. I remember you always wanted to be a fireman."

I nodded. "My dream came true."

He insisted on whipping up a batch of my favorite fruit tarts while we finished our tour. We got to the wall of photos and I pointed to the painted portrait of my father. "Every Kentucky Governor is on this wall." Then I pointed to the wall on the opposite side of the door. "And every first lady has her photo on that wall."

Brielle took her time perusing each portrait. "So much history," she commented.

"Yes. That's one thing we take very serious here: our history. At least in my family, but that may have more to do with my father's status." I thought about the millions of dollars' worth of Paul Sawyier paintings hanging on the mansion walls and the countless antiques with southern historical significance.

She stopped at a painting of Daniel Boone.

"He's a celebrity in Frankfurt. He's buried here in town."

She nodded. "He was a slave owner."

That got me thinking. "Yes. He was." I was ashamed to admit that I'd never thought twice about Boone owning slaves, but that's not to say that I condoned it.

Brielle sighed. "My father and I dug deep into our genealogy one summer during college. Turns out I have ancestors who were slaves."

"I'm so sorry." It seemed like a frivolous thing to say, but I didn't know how else to respond. Brielle was the first woman of color I'd dated and I hadn't considered how her race would give her a different perspective being in the south. I felt like a fool.

She put her hands on her hips as she moved to the next painting. "It's a part of our history as Americans—I get that—and I know there are important lessons to be learned from it, but I struggle with the glorification of figureheads who owned slaves."

I crossed my arms. "I can fully understand that." While Daniel Boone had done a lot for the development of Kentucky, his being a slave owner was rarely talked about. I tried to put myself in Brielle's shoes.

"Do you know the story of how Daniel Boone and some of his men were captured by the Shawnee Indians?"

I nodded. "Yeah. He negotiated their release and ended up being adopted into the tribe."

"And did you know that one of the men who helped negotiate his release was an ex-slave?"

I ran my hand over my chin. "No, I didn't."

"If my memory serves me correctly, I believe his name was

Pompey. He translated between Boone and the Shawnee. Pompey helped Boone vouch for his life to the Chief."

"And yet Boone is the hero, while Pompey has gone forgotten."

She nodded. "Precisely."

I reached for her hand. "I'm sorry it didn't occur to me that showing you all of this could be hurtful. And I feel like an idiot for never having thought of it that way until you pointed it out."

She squeezed my hand. "Our country has a long way to go. But these conversations—like the one you and I are having right now—that's the start of change."

She was right, there were important history lessons to be learned from these figures in our past, but we didn't need to put slave owners up on pedestals. Hell, there was a Boone and Bourbon Festival every summer in Frankfurt. I made a mental note to discuss this further with my father.

I kissed her forehead. "Let's go back to the kitchen. You're going to love Brady's fruit tarts. They're legendary."

After indulging in dessert, there was one last stop to make, and that was to the resident florist and decorator. I knocked on Fiona's door and she opened it promptly. She blinked rapidly before pulling me in for one of her famous hugs. "Why, Keith Hart, what on earth are you doin' gracing my door?"

I had fond memories of working with her when I'd been a kid in the Mansion. "I'm here for Christmas and I wanted to show my girlfriend where I grew up." I introduced Brielle.

"Fiona taught me everything I know about decorating for Christmas," I admitted.

The older woman blushed.

Brielle said to her, "You taught him well. We put up the most spectacular Christmas tree in our apartment this year because of him."

"He's always had an eye for beauty." Fiona winked.

After our visit, we left the Governor's Mansion and went back to the car. The sun was setting and it was perfect timing for our final stop. I pulled into the Buffalo Trace Distillery and Brielle just about pressed her face against the window. "What is this?" she exclaimed.

"The distillery does drive-thru Christmas lights on their property every year." I tuned the radio to the assigned station and we drove through as all of the installations danced along to the music. Brielle clutched my hand while we crept through the property, admiring all of the lights: flying reindeer, working elves, Santa, and a nativity scene. And there was no other person on the planet that I'd rather have in my passenger seat.

TWELVE

BRIELLE

Christmas Eve at the Hart mansion was something else. Not only did I feel like I was walking through a museum, but the staff outnumbered us, which seemed entirely too excessive. We sat down for an early dinner in the grand dining hall. The table was adorned with a pine green linen and a velvet red table runner. There was a Christmas tree in the corner (one of several in the house) and the fireplace was draped in garland and lights.

The chef and sous chef came out with trays of various southern dishes. There was mac and cheese, cornbread stuffing, collard greens, grits, black eyed peas, and an entire turkey fit for an army. While traditionally southern, it felt more like comfort food and I hadn't been expecting that given the lavishness of everything else.

After saying grace, we dug in. It was exorbitant, but oh so delicious. The chef had truly outdone himself and I fully understood why Keith had never learned to cook—especially after touring the Governor's Mansion, which had been another surreal experience. Besides, I can't really say I was surprised. The whole thing was very Lemon Hart. I'd gone in while the staff had been setting the table and snuck a peak at the underside of one of the dinner plates. They were handmade in France and were incredibly delicate. Made of porcelain and edged with actual gold, they had to be the most opulent plates I'd ever eaten off of. I was afraid to look up how much they were worth. Needless to say, I was extremely careful with using my knife. The silverware was heavy and shined like a mirror. Mrs. Hart mentioned that the set had been in her family for three generations.

Try as I might, imagining an aristocratic version of Keith was difficult. He was easily one of the most down-to-earth people I knew. On more than one occasion, he and I had eaten popcorn out of the microwave bag while watching a movie in our living room wearing pajamas. Most of the time, he rocked his bed-head hair and wore jeans and firehouse t-shirts. The only time I caught glimpses of the fancier Keith was when he got dressed up to go out somewhere nice, and while I quite enjoyed admiring that man all cleaned up in a suit, I still caught glimpses of the easy-going man I adored. Christmas Keith was certainly nice to look at. He wore crimson houndstooth dress pants with a black sweater over a white collared button-down. I didn't know Keith even owned anything houndstooth, but he certainly wore it well.

The rest of Keith's family, Blair included, fit the mold to perfection, but I struggled to see how Keith had ever been one of them. While he certainly could play the part when he absolutely had to, it was painfully obvious that it wasn't genuinely who he was. At least to me. It seemed his parents were in denial about that.

As if she could tell I'd been thinking about her, Mrs. Hart said, "Brielle, my dear friend Millicent wished for me to give you her regards."

I appreciated that the news producer had expressed an interest in helping to further my career, but I wasn't going to leverage my boyfriend's family for my own gain. And I definitely had no plans of moving to D.C. simply to appease the Harts' selfish need to get their son to move. They could try all they wanted, but Keith would never leave the FDNY. It was a big part of who he was, and I deplored that his parents would ever ask him to give it up.

In an effort to be polite, I replied, "That's very sweet of her. Please tell Millicent hello back for me."

"Why, of course." Mrs. Hart smirked. "We never finished our conversation yesterday in regards to children. With Corbett and Blair having their first would it not be wonderful to have cousins close in age?"

There was a limit to how polite I could be and Lemon Hart was dancing on that line. I put a forkful of turkey into my mouth to delay having to answer. Thankfully, Keith picked it up. "Don't push, Mother. We will not be pressured into having kids on your timeline. As I said yesterday, I want to make lieutenant first and Brielle's career is really starting to take off. Now is not the time for children. Besides, don't you want me to get married first?"

Mrs. Hart took a sip of her Pinot Noir, then looked directly at me. "Bless your heart, sugar. It is not easy being a career woman and a mother. That is what family is for. When Blair has the baby, I am going to take care of the child so that she can go back to work."

I swallowed in an attempt to hide my horror at the thought of Lemon Hart raising my child. "That's very generous of you, Mrs. Hart."

"Yes, well being around family is important." Her blue eyes darted to Keith before returning to me. "Would you not agree?"

As far as manipulation went, she was a master. To her credit, the woman was relentless.

"It is. That being said, I don't have the pleasure of being able to see my family too often, but we're still very close."

Keith crossed his silverware on his plate then placed his hand on my thigh. "Mother, stop trying to use Brielle to get me to move to D.C."

Senator Hart chimed in, "Speaking of your parents, Brielle, I had the pleasure of discovering some of their work. They are rather impressive."

I nodded. "Thank you, Senator."

"I'd love to arrange to meet them once they return from London."

My intuition panged in my gut. Regardless, I said, "I'm sure they'd like to meet you as well." My parents could handle themselves. They'd see through the Harts just like I had.

"Splendid."

AFTER DINNER, Keith and I went for a stroll around the property. We both desperately needed to walk off that meal and, while it went unsaid, we needed to put some distance between us and his parents. I bundled up in my winter gear, although it wasn't quite as cold as it was back home, and we headed for the empty pasture.

"You're a saint, Elle."

I cocked my head. "What do you mean?"

"I have to put up with my parents because I'm related to them, but you have voluntarily agreed to spend seven whole days with them in one month."

"Technically, you had coerced me into the first three days in D.C. without telling me what I was getting myself into until it was too late." I'd meant it as a joke, but his expression turned serious and he tucked his hands into the pockets of his coat.

"True. Sorry about that."

"No need to apologize. I was joking with you."

He sighed. "I guess I've gotten so used to their shit it has pretty much stopped bothering me. That's bad, right?"

My heart broke for him. "You should never be accepting of what they put you through. You deserve better."

He shrugged. "I can handle it. But I hate watching them try to do it to you, too."

I wiggled my arm between his elbow and his ribcage, hooking on to him. "I can handle myself, too."

"I know you can. That's not what I meant."

"Keith, your parents will never be able to use me to get to you. I can promise you that."

He smiled down at me. "What'd I tell you? You're a saint."

I laughed it off and we walked around the wooden horse fence in silence for a while until we arrived at the stable in the back paddock. Keith opened the door for me and we went inside to get away from the chill of the wind for a bit. It was smaller than the main barn and still held a faint smell of horses even though Keith had told me it'd been years since they'd been occupied.

I leaned against one of the stall doors while Keith stood in front of me and reached for my hips. I'd practically forgotten what our lives had been like a few weeks ago when we'd never touched in more than a friendly way. It simply felt right having him near like this.

He gave me a sweet, gentle kiss. "Can I ask you something?"

"Anything."

"Do you want kids?"

I hadn't expected that. I nodded. "One day. Yeah. Do you?"

"Eventually, yes."

I grinned. The idea of little humans running around that were half me and half Keith made my heart swell. "That's good."

He tucked a strand of hair behind my ear. "But I want to do it right. Get married. Be set in my career. Maybe even buy a place in the suburbs with a yard."

"The 'burbs, huh?" I teased. Keith may have grown up in the country, but he had become a city boy.

He leaned his forehead against mine. "One day."

"One day," I echoed.

His lips dusted mine. "I want that for us. Is it too soon to say that?"

Warmth spread through my body. "I want that, too."

His kiss was slow and we took our time exploring one another. His hands tangled in my hair and my gloved hands rested on his lower back, holding him against me. The coldness of his nose and lips was in stark contrast to the warmth of his breath and his tongue. I wondered if I'd ever tire of kissing Keith, but had a strong suspicion that wouldn't be possible. He had a way of making me feel special and beautiful and confident just from the way his lips claimed mine.

"Elle," he whispered against me when he came up for air.

"Yes?" I whispered back.

"Do you think it's too cold out here for us to—"

"No." I didn't need him to finish the question. My need for him outweighed the threat of being cold and I trusted him to keep me warm. After ditching my gloves, my fingers went for his belt buckle while his slid up my stockings and under my skirt. After what had happened to my tights that first night, I'd learned my lesson and switched to stockings

I dropped his pants to his knees and rubbed over the hardness straining against his boxer briefs. My hand threaded through the opening in the front of his underwear and pulled his shaft out. I loved how he was always hard and ready for me from the mere mention of sex. I stroked his length and he groaned as he continued to grow in my palm.

I jolted when his finger slipped beneath the crotch of my panties and plunged directly inside of me without warning. It was cold and sent a shiver through me. I clenched his digit with my walls, warming it quickly, then he added another cold finger making me shiver again as he thrust them into me.

"Fuck, Elle, you're dripping."

I swiped my thumb over his tip which was beading with pre-cum. "So are you," I replied, then licked him off of my fingertip.

His fingers stilled and his lips parted. "You're so incredibly sexy." He kissed me with an urgency as he increased the pace with his fingers.

He trapped my lip between his teeth making me exhale sharply, then he pulled back. The moonlight streaming through the stall slats gave us just enough light so I could see the copper in his eyes being swallowed up by his black pupils.

"Turn around," he ordered.

I let go of him and spun so that I was facing the stall.

Keith reached around and grabbed my wrists then brought them up to the bars on the top half of the door. "Hold on and don't let go."

My fingers wrapped around the cold metal bars and held on tight. He flipped my skirt up, exposing me to him and his hand rubbed against my backside, then he pulled away and as I was about to turn around and ask where he was going, his hand came down on my ass cheek making me yelp. My cold skin made the slap burn more than usual, but he quickly rubbed the spot with his palm to warm it.

Then he did it again. I was prepared for it this time and a

pleasurable sensation jolted through me. While I loved it when Keith was tender as he made love to me, it drove me wild when he got rough and fucked me. Knowing that's what he was priming to do, the excitement within me bubbled over.

He slapped my other cheek several times, always rubbing the spot afterward, then his shaft slid against my crack. "I fucking love this ass," he said, his deep voice even deeper than usual, as he beat his heavy cock against me.

I moaned. "Please, Keith."

"Please, Keith, what?"

"I want you."

"What do you want?"

I'd never been vocal when it came to sex, but Keith was always making me talk to him. Seeing how much it turned him on helped some of my reservations slip away. "I want you to fuck me."

His fingers danced around my entrance. "You want my dick in this pussy?"

"Yes."

He leaned forward and growled in my ear. "Tell me."

"Give it to me."

He lined his head up with my opening. "Is this what you want, baby?"

"Yes," I choked out. My desire was getting the best of me.

He slipped his head inside of me and then pulled it back out with a pop.

I cried out, "No. Come back."

Again, he slid his head into me and retreated.

I whimpered.

He did it again.

"More," I begged.

Again, in and out.

"More what?" The words trembled through his teeth. He was torturing himself just as much as he was torturing me.

"I need you to fuck me."

He slipped the tip in again and paused. I could tell he wanted to keep torturing me until he was fully satisfied with my words, but he needed me too. The way his fingers dug into my hips made that perfectly clear.

I gave him what he wanted to hear. "Give it to me. Fuck my pussy with your hard cock, Keith." He always got off on hearing me say his name.

He plunged deep inside and we both gasped as his balls bounced against me. After taking all of a second to acclimate, he retreated and slammed into me again.

And again.

And again.

Faster.

And faster.

The moans fell from my lips to his rhythm.

He wrapped a hand around my stomach to keep me from moving away from him as he continued to fuck out all of his frustration.

My legs began to tremble as my orgasm built and I clenched my walls around him.

He pounded into me harder.

I clenched.

Harder still.

My body shook. "Yes! Don't stop, don't stop," I begged as my orgasm took hold and I spiraled off in ecstasy.

At some point, I'd let go of the stall bars and my shoulder was pressed against the door. Keith's torso leaned against my back and his arms were wrapped around my midsection, practically holding me up. My legs felt like jelly and threatened to give out. They probably already had, which would explain why Keith was supporting my body as he drilled into me.

He felt so damn good. The friction built up and I quickly approached a second orgasm. The way the curve of Keith's head hit my g-spot in this position, I could have an endless stream of orgasms.

I pushed my palms against the door as Keith continued to rail me from behind. My breaths were quick and shallow as the pressure increased inside me and I clenched my muscles around his shaft.

"Oh, fuck," he uttered. He was getting close, too.

"Come with me," I said as I felt the beginning flutter of my release.

He thrust faster and I screamed as my body shook with pleasure again. Suddenly, he slowed and roared as he shot his load inside.

We were both hot and panting. Keith squeezed my ass as he pulled out of me. "Shit," he exclaimed. "Shit, shit."

"What is it?" I straightened up and as I did so, juices dripped down my thigh. A lot of it. We'd forgotten the condom. "Oh." I knew it had felt a little too good.

"I'm sorry. I'm sorry." He frantically inserted a finger into me, curled it, and pulled it back out.

"What are you doing?"

"Trying to get my cum out."

I swatted his hand away and tried to stifle a laugh, but it was no use. "That's not going to work."

"I can't believe I forgot. I'm so sorry, Elle."

I wasn't on the pill because I'd heard too many horror stories. In my head, I tried to calculate where I was in my cycle. My last period came our last day in D.C., which meant I shouldn't have ovulated yet. Chance of me getting pregnant was low, but it was still a possibility. *Damn.* "It's not a big deal. I'll go get the morning after pill."

His tight shoulders released a little. "Right. Smart thinking."

Then it dawned on me what day it was. "Umm, pharmacies here are open on Christmas, right?"

The tension returned to his shoulders. "I—I don't know."

That was problematic. New York spoiled us. Holiday, late night, early morning—didn't matter. You could get just about anything 24/7 in Manhattan.

"I'll look it up. If there isn't one in Frankfort, I'm sure there'll be one in Louisville that's open. I can drive there first thing and get it for you."

Louisville was the city we had flown into. It was nearly an hour away. That would suck, but at least it was an option.

Keith pulled a handkerchief from his pocket and handed it to me.

"Thanks." I cleaned myself up, put the handkerchief into my coat pocket, then smoothed my skirt back down. By then, he was buckling his belt. I located my gloves that had been discarded on the ground and put them back on.

When I looked up, he was staring at me with tender eyes. "What is it?" I asked.

He cupped my cheek. "That was fun. Sorry I ruined it."

I rolled onto my toes and gave him a peck on the lips. "You didn't ruin it. We're going to take care of that. Plus, I enjoyed myself."

He gave me a lopsided grin. "We should probably head back."

I took his extended hand and we made our way to the house. Corbett was in the less formal living room in the back of the house talking with Mrs. Hart. Blair had already gone to bed. The pregnancy was apparently zapping up a lot of her energy. The senator was nowhere to be seen.

I wanted to properly clean myself up before joining in any conversations—I was convinced I smelled of sex. And maybe even a little bit like horses. Keith must've had the same idea because he followed me upstairs to his bedroom. After stripping off my coat and gloves, I retrieved the handkerchief from my pocket and brought it with me to the en suite bathroom so I could rinse it out.

While I was doing that, Keith came walking in wearing only his underwear. My thighs clenched together at the sight. He jumped in the shower and was done in less than a minute.

Wrapped in a towel, he came up behind me at the sink and kissed my head. "I'm going to find my father. There's something I have to talk to him about. Come on down when you're through?"

I nodded. "Okay."

He kissed my head again and left me to do my thing. Once I was finished, I spent a few minutes mentally preparing myself for another socially awkward conversation with Keith's family before leaving the bedroom.

I went back downstairs and was craving a cup of tea, so I headed toward the kitchen to ask the staff if they had any. On my way there, I approached Senator Hart's office and noticed the door was cracked and the lights were on. As I got closer, I heard voices.

"I understand." That was Keith.

I knew I shouldn't eavesdrop, but curiosity got the best of me.

The Senator said, "Good. I am proud of you son. Brielle is perfect. Having a grandchild with African American blood will be very useful for my Presidential campaign."

My breath hitched in my throat.

Silence.

I waited for Keith to tell him off.

After a beat, my *boyfriend* replied, "Thank you, Colonel."

And my heart broke in two.

He'd had me completely fooled. Forgetting the condom *hadn't* been an accident. I guess he really was Lemon Hart's son, after all.

I needed to get the hell out of Kentucky. History was repeating itself, except this time the betrayal cut so much deeper. I had cared about Mitchell, but I loved Keith. Hell, I was in love with him.

And he'd been playing me.

I had been nothing more to him than a pawn in his family's political game.

My skin was still tingling from the hot-as-fuck sex with my girlfriend as I headed down the hall toward my father's office. Before Brielle and I had gone on our walk, the Colonel had pulled me aside and asked if he could talk to me privately, so after my shower, I went to meet with him.

I knocked on the door.

"Enter."

I twisted the glass knob and pushed the door in. My father was leaning on his large cherry wood desk with a notebook in his hand.

"You wanted to see me?" I pushed the door behind me, but it didn't close all the way. Instead of bothering to go back, I continued inside until I was standing by my father.

"Yes." He placed the notebook on the desk beside him before removing his reading glasses, which he then dangled from his fingers.

"You are a valued member of this family, son."

I tried not to roll my eyes. Politics 101: When you're about to tell someone something they won't like, always start by complimenting them.

He continued, "As you know, when someone is a political figure, their family is as well simply because of association."

I tucked my hands into my pockets, wishing he'd get straight to the point. "Right..." I dragged out the vowel.

"As you are also aware, I plan on taking a run at the presidency."

I nodded.

"When I do, this family will be expected to step up."

I sighed. "You know I'll support you, Colonel. D.C. isn't a far drive from New York. I'll come down for what I have to." I'd hate it, but I would. For all his flaws, my father was a good politician. I wanted his dreams to come true, even if he didn't want the same for me.

He placed his glasses down on top of his notebook. "I'd like you to move to Washington."

I hadn't expected him to come right out and say it; it wasn't political if you weren't dancing around what you meant all of the time, but if he was going to be blunt, then so was I. "Not going to happen. I'm sorry you don't approve of what I do, but I'm not leaving my career. And I'm not leaving New York."

His lips tightened. "The next race is in two years. I'll be announcing my intent to run this January."

I took a deep breath. This was a big deal. Having always been a politician's son, I knew what that would entail. "Congratulations. I know how much this means to you."

He dipped his chin. "Thank you. I'm going to need your support in this."

"And you'll have it."

He nodded. "Your image will be just as important as mine. And that will extend beyond *you*."

I ran a hand over my chin. He was talking about Brielle.

We'd both have to toe the line...to an extent. My heart ached. If she couldn't handle that, I didn't know what I'd do. I wet my lips. "I understand."

"Good." He grinned. "I am proud of you son. Brielle is perfect. Having a grandchild with African American blood will be very useful for my Presidential campaign."

My father's words hit me like a shockwave. I blinked a few times as I tried to get a hold of the anger rising to my throat. I actually tried to tell myself I hadn't heard him correctly, but I knew I had.

My nostrils flared. "Thank you, Colonel."

"You're welcome."

"No." Clearly my sarcasm had gone over his head. "Thank you for making this decision easy for me." I stepped toward him and he stood so we were face-to-face. I threatened in a hushed tone. "Stay the hell away from me and Brielle you racist son of a bitch."

"How dare you speak to me like that," he spat. "Welcoming a black girl into *my* family is far from racist."

"If you believe that, then you have some serious work to do on educating yourself." I lifted a finger inches from his face. "And leveraging *my child* for your own gain is low. Even for you. I'll say this one last time. Stay the hell away from me. I'm done with your politics. I'm done with this dysfunctional fucking family. And I am done with you." I turned on my heels and charged out of the room, ignoring his shouts behind me.

I needed to find Brielle and get out of there, so I went by the living room expecting to see her in there with Mother and Corbett, but she wasn't. Thinking maybe she was still in our bedroom, I flew up the steps, taking two at a time. The door was open and when I went inside, and I immediately noticed that her luggage was missing.

What the fuck?

"Elle?" I called out as I went to check the bathroom, but it was empty, too, and her makeup bag was gone from the counter. I stepped into the hallway. "Brielle?"

Nothing.

My cell phone was charging on my night stand so I went to get it to call her. When I picked it up, a piece of paper was sitting beneath it.

Don't follow me, Keith.

I collapsed onto the bed and fumbled to unlock my phone through my shaking hands. After finding her name, I hit the call button. It rang through to her voicemail. Bile rose to my throat. *This can't be happening.* I tried again with the same result.

I went to the closet and dragged my suitcase out, then tossed in my things all while continuously calling her and willing her to pick up.

After zipping my bag, I hauled ass down the stairs. Forgetting I didn't have a car, I cursed under my breath. Taking one from my parents wasn't going to happen. Then I remembered that Corbett had driven there from D.C. because Blair didn't like to fly.

I dropped my suitcase by the door and charged into the living room. The Colonel was in there, no doubt detailing our conversation to the rest of the family.

"Corbett, I need your car keys."

He scrunched up his face. "What?"

"Your keys. Now. I need your keys. It's an emergency."

My mother butt in. "Darling, take a moment and think about this."

I ignored her.

Corbett dug into his pocket and pulled them out then

walked over to me. In a soft enough tone to keep our parents from hearing, he asked, "What's going on?"

The adrenaline from my fear was making me shake. I quietly replied, "Brielle is gone. I think she went to the airport and I have to stop her. But I don't have a car."

My father threatened, "Corbett, do not give him those keys. You are not going anywhere, Keith. We have to talk."

My brother handed me his keys. "Good luck. Keep me posted." He'd pay for that, but I didn't have time to worry about the retribution.

"I will," I replied, then I ran from the room, picked up my bag and sprinted for the driveway.

While I raced to Louisville, I continued to call Brielle. When I reached the interstate, the call didn't ring. It went straight to voicemail. She must've turned it off.

"Fuck," I screamed as I punched the steering wheel.

I pushed the gas a little harder. After wracking my brain trying to figure out what the hell had happened, I came up with nothing other than maybe she was mad because I'd forgotten to wear a condom, but I thought I'd been more upset about it. At least that's how it had seemed.

Everything had been fine while we were in the bathroom all of twenty minutes ago. What could have happened between then and now? And then it clicked. Mother.

Brielle had probably gone down to sit with my family while I talked to the Colonel and Mother had probably said something out of line. I knew Brielle's patience had been wearing thin and it wouldn't have taken much for my mother to push the right buttons and shove her over the edge. If my mother had cost me Brielle, I'd never forgive her.

I screamed through my teeth, hating myself for thinking subjecting Brielle to four days with my family was a good idea. I'd been selfish asking her to go with me. That wasn't fair of me.

It's just that I didn't want to leave her—especially not on Christmas.

As I raced toward the airport, I realized that I needed a plan. We weren't scheduled to fly out for another two days. If Brielle was going home, she'd have to change her flight. She was smart, she wouldn't go to the airport and hope to get lucky enough to get put right on a plane. No, she'd call ahead and change her flight.

After unlocking my phone, I called the airline and jammed my finger against the zero to bypass the automated system and get a live person on the phone.

"Thank you for calling USA Air. This call is being recorded for training and quality purposes. My name is Nancy. May I have your name please?"

"Keith Hart." I tried to sound calm though I was anything but.

"Hello, Mr. Hart. How may I assist you this evening?"

"My gi—wife had to change her return flight from Louisville to New York and I forgot to write the new flight information down. Could you look it up for me please?"

I had booked the flights for us, so luckily the reservations were connected and I hoped that was enough to get the woman to give me the information I needed.

"Absolutely. What is the reservation number?"

"I'm driving and don't have it readily available. Can you look it up another way?"

"Sure. What is Mrs. Hart's first name?"

I was pretty sure that giving out other people's information over the phone wasn't allowed, so maybe saying she was my wife would help my case.

"Uh, it's Brielle Jackson. She hasn't changed her last name yet."

The woman tapped on the keyboard. "Yes, I see Keith Hart and Brielle Jackson."

"Yes, that's it."

"Hmm. It appears that your wife called and canceled her flight. She didn't re-book with us."

The blood drained from my face. "Are you sure she didn't just book under a new reservation?"

More keyboard tapping. "I'm sorry, Mr. Hart, but I can't provide you with another passenger's information if you're not on the same reservation."

I held back a scream. "Okay.

"Is there anything else I can help you with, Mr. Hart?"

"No."

"Thank you for calling USA Air and have—"

Click.

I called Brielle's phone again praying that maybe she had been going through a dead zone before instead of having turned it off. Straight to voicemail. This time, I left a message. "Elle, what is going on? I called the airline and they said you canceled your flight, but you didn't rebook. Where are you? Why did you leave? What did I do? Whatever it is, I'm sorry. Please don't do this." I choked back emotion. "Don't leave me. I'm on my way to the airport. If you're there, please wait for me. Let's talk about whatever this is. Please, baby." I inhaled a shaky breath. "I love you."

I hung up. That certainly wasn't how I'd imagined telling her I loved her for the first time, but I was desperate. She had to know just how much she meant to me. Fuck, I'd just renounced my family for her. And I would do it again in a heartbeat. She was my world.

No way was I letting her go. Not without laying it all out there. Not without a fight. And sure as hell not without finding out what had made her leave.

I arrived at the Lexington airport just in time to catch the final flight of the evening. It was going to Newark, NJ but I didn't care—I'd make it work. I had to get home as soon as possible. Hurrying down the jet bridge, I kept checking over my shoulder for Keith, but he never appeared. Once on board, I sank into my seat and let out a deep breath allowing some of my anxiety to melt away. A few minutes later, the door closed and we were in the air.

After having overheard the conversation between Keith and his father, I had gone straight to the bedroom, thrown my things into my bag, and put on my sneakers so I could move faster. Thankfully, the family had been in the back of the house, so none of them had seen me sneak out the door. As I had jogged down the ridiculously long driveway, I'd called for an Uber, but the driver had been twenty minutes away. A far cry from Manhattan. By that time, Keith would have likely found my note, which I knew he'd disobey, and I did not want him to find me. I almost hadn't left a note, but despite my anger,

I still loved the asshole and it had felt like the right thing to do rather than disappear without a word.

I'd called the driver and told him to meet me on the road, then I had slung my luggage over my shoulder and sprinted down the driveway. When I had made it to the street, I'd turned left because surely, Keith would take a right out of the driveway as that was the way to the airport.

Once the house had been out of view, I'd slowed to a walk. I'd never been more grateful for all of the cardio my trainer made me do. As I'd waited for the car, I'd pulled flights up on my phone. There wasn't one out of Louisville until the morning and even if I spent the night in a hotel, undoubtedly, Keith would be waiting for me on that flight. I couldn't imagine anything worse than being trapped thirty-thousand feet in the air for hours with the man who'd cut my heart out.

I'd remembered Keith saying there was another airport that was smaller nearby, so I'd looked up that one. Lexington was much closer—only a thirty-minute drive—and it was in the complete opposite direction of Louisville, which was good because Keith would be driving an hour-and-a-half in the wrong direction. He'd been blowing up my phone, so he'd obviously found my note.

Once in the car, I'd called the airline to cancel my existing flight so I could book the new one under my name, which meant Keith would be none the wiser. After I'd gotten everything arranged, I turned off my phone so that I didn't have to keep silencing Keith's calls.

Apparently, in addition to his mother's manipulation skills, he'd also inherited her relentlessness.

I closed my eyes and listed to the roar of the jet engines, trying desperately not to cry. Keith was one of my best friends —had been for years—and I couldn't believe he'd betray me like that. I'd gone through the whole Mitchell fiasco prior to meeting Keith, so he didn't know what had gone down with that. I wondered, if he had, if he still would've targeted me. Did he care about me even that much? I squeezed my eyelids tightly and took a few steadying breaths. I would not lose it on an airplane.

The emotional pain was becoming physical. My head was pounding and my chest ached. Had it all been a lie? Or had he seen an opportunity arise that he couldn't pass up? Either way, I must not have ever meant anything to him. I didn't know whether to be impressed with his acting skills or sickened by them. Truthfully, I was a little of both.

Growing up on Long Island, I had been one of six black kids in my class. For the most part, they'd stuck together. I say *they* because I was mixed raced, which somehow made me a misfit. Traveling as much as I had hadn't helped me find my clique. I had friends, sure, but I'd always been coming and going, which had made it difficult for me to fit in. My friends had spanned across groups, which in retrospect had been a good thing. I hadn't been pigeon-holed.

My life in London had been different. My school had been more diverse and the students hadn't self-segregated. The color of one's skin hadn't mattered there. It's not that discrimination had been an overt problem at my school in the States, more like the students had chosen to stick with those who had been like them.

As an adult, I was grateful to have had both of those experiences. I'd learned that racism isn't always obvious, but it still existed here. I think that's one reason I really admire my parents. In their careers, they'd both fought uphill battles. My father's battle had been the color of his skin and my mother's had been her gender. Despite that, they'd both managed to create very successful careers for themselves.

Another thing I admired was their commitment to each

other. They entered into an interracial relationship thirty years ago, and I knew it couldn't have been easy. For the most part, they'd shielded me from the criticism, but I remembered one particular incident at the grocery store when I was five or six. We'd gone as a family, but my mom had waited in the car—I don't remember why—and I had been holding my father's hand while we shopped. I'm fairly light-skinned and I'm sometimes confused for being Spanish, plus I have a lot of my mom's features, so people are surprised that my dad is my father.

A middle-aged white woman in a long fur coat had been following us around the grocery store. When we'd gotten to the checkout line, my mom had come inside and she'd joined us. My father had kissed her on the forehead to greet her and I'd noticed the woman had gotten in the line beside us with a man who'd I'd assumed to be her husband. The look of disgust on the woman's face when my dad had kissed my mom was something I'll never forget. Then, her husband said something to her along the lines of "dirtying the gene pool."

I'd felt my father stiffen, but he hadn't commented in return. The ride home after that had been extra quiet. When we'd gotten back to the house, my parents had told me to go play in my room, but I hovered in the hallway instead and I'd overheard them talking to my grandparents in the kitchen.

Mom had said something like, "Will the hate ever end?"

To which my Nan had replied, "No. I'd like to think that it will, but that's not realistic. I hope it'll get better, but it'll never go away completely. That's why we have to teach that daughter of yours where she came from. Mark my words, it's her generation that'll demand change."

I never forgot that.

They never made me define myself. I honored my white side and I honored my black side. On forms, I checked both the Caucasian and the African American boxes. My parents had taught me about my ancestry and I was as proud to be the descendant of slaves as I was to be a descendant of the British aristocracy—I had a great-great grandfather who had been a Baron. I lived with my dad's parents in the States, and whenever we were in London I spent a lot of time with my mom's parents. I've always straddled the line and I was grateful for that. It made me a much stronger person.

Having spent the time I had with Keith's family, I realized how blessed I was to have been born into my family—for many reasons. For Senator Hart to say he'd want to use Keith's and my potential child as a way to win over the black vote truly made me sick to my stomach. And to know that Keith had been a part of that plan was unforgivable.

The guy beside me started snoring. I still had a long night ahead of me after the three-and-a-half-hour flight, so I tried to push aside all of my anger and get some sleep. Eventually, I drifted off and woke up as we made our approach into Newark. I'd carried my bag on the plane, so I didn't have to wait at the carousel. After disembarking, I went straight for the rental car counter. Forgetting that it was one of the busiest travel times of the year, I had some serious sticker shock when the guy at customer service told me how much a rental would be. They'd hiked the prices up and all they had left were luxury vehicles. It would've cost me a fortune, especially since I'd be returning the car to a different location, so I decided to take a car service instead.

Half-an-hour later, I was home. But it no longer felt safe to me. My boyfriend/best friend/roommate was not the person I'd thought he was. And his father was complete scum. I couldn't stay in that apartment. Since moving out at midnight wasn't a feasible option, I packed as much as I could into the couple of suitcases I owned and turned on my phone to call a car service to come get me and bring me to my parents' house on Long

Island. Since they were gone until the middle of January, I'd be able to stay there by myself until I figured out where I was going to live. Commuting into the city for work would be brutal. I'd have to wake up at three in the morning, but I had no other choice.

The voicemail icon displayed in my notifications and I didn't have to look to know who it was from. There were also text messages. I didn't have the energy to deal with that, so I tucked my phone into my purse and stared out the car window for the next thirty-minutes until we pulled up to my childhood home. It was nearly two in the morning by the time I was able to lay my head down on my pillow in the room I'd grown up in. Way past my bed time. Yet, I couldn't sleep. Instead, I finally let myself cry.

I hugged my pillow and let it all out. My boyfriend's—ex-boyfriend's—family was using me as their token black girl. And the man I loved was complicit in their plan by knocking me up. The betrayal was agonizing and my body heaved as sobs overtook me.

It seemed like forever had passed by the time I stopped crying. I went to the bathroom to blow my nose and my reflection in the mirror was ghastly. The whites of my eyes were red and my upper and lower eyelids were swollen and pink. I had bags under my eyes and my skin was sallow. At three-thirty in the morning, I decided to take a shower. I made the water as hot as I could tolerate and tried to wash away all of my pain as I scrubbed the memory of Keith from my body.

My skin was practically raw by the time I was done. I lathered on my lotion and got back into bed. I tossed and turned for another hour. Out of frustration, I gave in and, against my better judgment, decided to check my messages. I pulled up the texts first.

Keith: I'm really worried. Where are you? Please answer me and just let me know that you're safe.

Keith: Please, Elle. Tell me what happened. I want to fix this. I need you. Please.

Keith: I'm freaking out. You don't have to talk to me, just please text me and say that you're safe.

Keith: I got a flight home in the morning. I'm hoping to see you at the airport. I promise I won't bother you. I just need to get my eyes on you and know that you're okay.

A tinge of guilt panged inside me, but I swallowed it down. He was faking it and it would do me right to remember he'd never really cared about me. I hesitated and took a deep breath before playing his voicemail: "Elle, what is going on? I called the airline and they said you canceled your flight, but you didn't rebook. Where are you? Why did you leave? What did I do? Whatever it is, I'm sorry. Please don't do this. Don't leave me. I'm on my way to the airport. If you're there, please wait for me. Let's talk about whatever this is. Please, baby. I love you."

Tears streamed down my face again. His voice was laced with emotion and I could tell he had been on the verge of tears. He was good. I almost believed the ruse. Hearing him say he loved me hurt. Badly. We'd never said those words to each other, but I'd felt them. For me, those feelings were real. The fact that he could use that phrase to try and manipulate me only proved that the man I thought I knew didn't exist. The real Keith Hart was callous and...heartless.

FIFTEEN

KEITH

Brielle hadn't been at the airport. I'd sat in the terminal the entire night and waited for her to show up, but she never did. I had called my mother and demanded to know what she'd done, but she'd said that she hadn't spoken to Brielle since before our walk. It made no fucking sense. Things had been fine when we'd gotten back to the house and I kept going over it all in my head, but couldn't for the life of me figure out what had happened.

When I got on the plane, I tried to call Brielle again, but got her voicemail. Worried wasn't a strong enough word to describe how I was feeling. I'd dry-heaved into the toilet at the airport the entire night. My stomach was in knots, the pressure behind my eyes was excruciating, and my fucking heart hurt. Like actually hurt.

At JFK airport, I hoped in a cab and fidgeted the entire drive back to my apartment—our apartment. Brielle's and mine. I flung the door open, leaving my suitcase in the foyer and shouted, "Brielle?"

I sprinted to her bedroom, finding the door open and the

room empty. I fell to my knees when I noticed her half-empty closet. She'd also left some of her dresser drawers ajar and they were empty as well.

I buried my face into my hands and cried. She'd left me. And I had no idea why. The past eighteen hours had taught me more about love than any other experience in my life ever had. A piece of me was dying inside and I felt powerless to stop it. Brielle had always been important to me and I'd loved her for a long time, but being *in love* with her was something entirely different.

I suspect I'd been unknowingly falling for her since she'd moved in with me. There's an intimacy that comes along with being roommates. Even though we had never been more than friends because I'd had a girlfriend, that hadn't stopped my heart from falling. Less than a month before, I'd finally acknowledged those feelings and there was no going back after that. Brielle was a part of me and she always would be—whether we were together or not.

I was slow to get to my feet. My body ached like I had the flu. I fished my phone from my pocket and pulled up Brielle's name to send a text.

Keith: I'm home and you aren't here. Obviously, you know that. I'm praying that you come back. Whenever you're ready. This is your home, Elle. Always will be. I don't know what I did wrong and it's killing me. You don't have to tell me where you are, but please just let me know that you're safe. I'm begging you.

I hit send and went to my room to collapse on my bed. I closed my eyes and prayed that she was all right.

My phone buzzed and I couldn't unlock it fast enough. Her name was on the screen.

Brielle: I'm safe

A weight lifted off my chest and I sighed heavily. *Thank you*, I offered up to the heavens.

Keith: Okay good. Thanks for letting me know.

I probably should have ended it there, so as to not push her, but I was desperate.

Keith: Can you tell me what made you leave? What did I do? I want to fix this, baby, but I can't if I don't know what happened.

I waited.
Ten minutes later, my phone buzzed again.

Brielle: There will be no fixing this because there is no this anymore. We're over. I'll move the rest of my stuff out next week. Don't bother contacting me again. I'm blocking your number.

The blow might as well have come from a shotgun. I curled into a ball as waves of pain rolled over me. *This can't be happening,* I repeated over and over in my head. This was the worst Christmas ever. No, not just Christmas—this was the worst day of my entire life.

IT HAD BEEN three days since I'd gotten back to New York and I hadn't heard a word from Brielle since her last text, nor had she come back to the apartment. I almost called in a favor to get out of work that day, but decided that running into a burning building and putting an ax through a wall would do me some good.

I'd kept to myself all morning and had insisted on doing the truck check so I could keep my mind occupied with anything other than Brielle. Once I'd finished, I plopped myself into a chair in the kitchen and stared at the wall. Jace and Dylan took the seats across from me.

Dylan asked, "What's going on?"

I shrugged. "Tired."

"Fuck that," Jace said. "I've seen you exhausted before and this isn't that."

Dylan shook his head. "Nope. This is heartbreak if I've ever seen it."

I hated my friends at that moment. The last thing I wanted to do was talk to anyone about Brielle.

"Spill it," Jace urged.

I drummed my fingers on the table.

"Look, bro, we've both been there. We know it sucks, but we got through it. Let us help." Dylan coaxed.

I wet my lips. "Brielle left me. She's gone."

"What happened?" Jace asked.

So I told them and when I was done, they both had sullen expressions.

Dylan ran a hand over his head. "And you have no idea what you did to piss her off?"

"No fucking clue."

Jace leaned back in his chair and crossed his arms. "Well, you need to find out."

I glared at him. "No shit. But how the hell am I supposed to do that if she won't talk to me?"

"Can you go see her at work?" Dylan suggested.

I shook my head. "I need a visitor's pass to get into the studio and she's not going to get me one."

"And you don't know where she's staying?" Jace asked.

"Nope. I'm assuming she's with a friend or maybe at her parents' house."

Jace scratched his chin. "Can you go by there?"

"I don't know the address." I was cursing myself for not insisting on a drive by of her childhood home that night we'd met her parents for dinner.

"Shit," Dylan uttered.

"Yeah."

"There's got to be a way," Jace insisted. "We're gonna figure this out."

The alarm went off and we sprung for our chairs to get on the rig. In less than a minute we were barreling out of the station and on our way to work.

I'd like to preface this by saying I don't wish a fire on anyone, but I was damn glad to be going to one. I needed the rush. Thick, black smoke was billowing out of the windows of the single-family attached-dwelling. I didn't even want to think about how many millions of dollars the place was worth. Single-family homes were hard to come by in Manhattan, so the few there were had an astronomical value.

A woman in a robe was standing out front waving frantically at us. Our lieutenant instructed us to do a primary search of the four-story brownstone, so when I hopped off the truck, I grabbed a set of irons—a Halligan and an ax—and charged into the building behind Dylan.

"Go left, go left," Dylan instructed as we entered the house into a reception room. He went right, and we met up on the other side to make our way to the next room.

Our radio squelched as we were passing the stairs. "Be

advised, there is an elderly woman in a bedroom on the second floor."

Without needing to say a word, we turned and went up the steps.

"Going up to the second," Dylan replied to our lieutenant.

The heat intensified significantly, forcing us to crawl, as we approached the top of the staircase. Heat rises in a fire, but for it to be that hot, I knew the fire was on this floor.

There were a decent number of brownstones in our area on the Upper West Side and they all tended to have similar layouts, which made our searches easier. We crawled down the hall to our right, leading us straight into the back bedroom. The smoke was thick and I couldn't see a damn thing, but I heard the crackle of the flames.

Dylan and I split the room again; he went right and I went left.

"Call out," I shouted, but got nothing in return.

I felt around the perimeter. I went from a dresser to a night stand meaning a bed was right in front of me. I brought my Halligan up and swiped it over the top of the bed hoping to bump into a victim, but it was empty. I repeated the same underneath the bed. Also vacant.

I met Dylan in the middle. "Anything?"

"No. Let's check the other room."

We crossed each other and I checked the side he had just gone through while he traced over my path. Then, we went back into the hall. There was a bathroom on the right, so I did a quick check, finding it empty, then we continued to the other bedroom.

Unmistakably, the fire was in there. Heat smacked into me like a dang brick wall.

"Call out," Dylan belted as we split the room.

A faint cough came from not far in front of me. I surged forward and found the victim slumped over in an armchair.

"Hogan, she's here." I got up onto my knees. "Ma'am I've got you." She was frail—I could feel her bones through my gloves.

Dylan snapped to my side. "Found the fire. We've got to get the fuck out of here."

"Call for a basket." Carrying her wasn't feasible because of the heat and dragging her could do more harm than good to her body.

Dylan hit his radio. "Fire located in the second-floor front bedroom. Found the victim. We need a Stokes Basket in here."

I wrapped my arms around the woman's chest and slid her to the floor. She was unconscious and barely breathing.

"On my way up with a basket," Jace said over the radio.

I had a bad fucking feeling. The kind where your gut tells you that something is about to go seriously wrong. "We've got to go."

"I'll meet him at the door," Dylan said before crawling away.

I hated to do it, but I had to drag the woman. We needed to move and every second counted. I grabbed onto her shirt beneath her shoulders and tried to get to my feet so I could pull her, but the heat immediately forced me back to my knees.

"Shit. Shit," I uttered as I retrieved the roll of webbing from my pants before racing to circle it around her body, tucking it beneath her arms and under her legs, before bringing the loops together and creating a harness with straps I could drag.

I gripped the webbing and tugged. I'd barely moved a foot when the house rumbled like a dang earthquake. "Oh, fuck," I shouted as I covered the woman's body with my own. Brielle's face popped into my head just before the ceiling came down around us.

Tired was an understatement. So was exhausted. I'd hardly slept in four days and I'd gotten on the train at four in the morning so I could make it to work on time. I desperately had to find a place to live in the city before that commute killed me.

I scrolled through my emails at my desk between shows, catching up on what I'd missed while I'd been away, but I struggled to concentrate. Since I had Keith's schedule, I knew he was at the firehouse, so I'd hired a moving company to meet me at my old apartment after work, that way I could get my stuff out while he was gone. Seeing him would've been too risky. As angry as I was, I couldn't bring myself to hate him because my stupid heart was still in love with the jerk and I didn't trust myself to be around him. While he wanted to have a conversation about what had happened, I wanted to move on. The sooner I put Keith Hart in the rearview, the better.

I'd spent the weekend licking my wounds and I went back and forth between crying over the loss of the man I loved and screaming with anger because of what he'd done and how stupid I'd been to fall for it. That first day, I'd stayed in bed for thirty-six hours, only getting up to use the bathroom and drink water. I hadn't eaten in days and my empty stomach protested with sharp pains, but every time I'd tried to eat, I couldn't bring myself to swallow.

It had taken extra long in makeup that morning to cover up the bags under my eyes and the sadness...everywhere. Fatima had been doing my hair and makeup since I'd started as an anchor at USBC and I knew she could tell I was going through something, but all she said was, "My grandmother always told me that after every storm, there's a rainbow, so keep your head up or you'll miss it."

It was exactly what I'd needed to hear. I wasn't the kind of person to gush about my personal life, and Fatima knew that, but that didn't mean I hadn't needed a little encouragement. Moving on without Keith would be one of the hardest things I've ever had to do. In one night, I'd lost my best friend and my roommate—which is hard enough—but also the man I loved. While I'd been through break ups before, nothing compared to the hole Keith left in my heart.

My desk phone rang. It was Shelby, one of the producers of the morning and noon show, summoning me to her office. It wasn't often that the producers needed to talk to me, and I wondered what it could possibly be about. Sure, I'd been a little off my game that morning when I'd reported on the post-Christmas retail surge in front of Macy's, but I hadn't thought it'd been bad enough to warrant being spoken to.

Her office door was open. "You wanted to see me?"

"Yes, Brielle. Close the door and have a seat." She gestured to the chairs in front of her desk and I took a seat.

She interlaced her fingers on top of the desk. "Are you happy here?"

Taken aback, I tilted my head. "Yes. Very much so."

Was I getting fired?

She nodded. "You know, if you aren't you could talk to me about it. I'd want you to talk to me about it."

I crossed my legs and rested my hands on my knee. "I will."

"Good. There's a producer from the USBC affiliate in Washington D.C. that has been asking around about you."

My stomach dropped. Millicent. "Oh."

"So, I'll ask again. Are you happy here?"

I clenched my fingers onto fists. "Yes. I'm definitely not interested in going to D.C." Even if I had been, that was certainly off the table after everything with Keith. "That's a big misunderstanding."

"All right. I'm glad to hear it. We'd hate to lose you."

I breathed out in relief.

"Now that we've cleared that up. I have a proposition for you. How would you like to co-host the network's New Year's Eve show?"

I couldn't possibly have heard her correctly. "As in the News at Noon show that day? Because I thought I was already doing that."

She grinned. "No, I mean *the* New Year's Eve show. From nine to midnight."

My eyes widened and my jaw hung open. "*The* New Year's Eve show? Like in Times Square? With the celebrity guests? And the countdown to the ball drop?"

Shelby's laugh told me she was enjoying my shock. "That's the one."

I scooted to the edge of my seat. "Are you serious?"

"Sure am. Hillary Pierson got appendicitis, so she can't do it and we need to replace her."

Hillary had been doing the show for the last decade. "And you want *me* to co-host?"

"Unless you don't want to."

"Yes, of course I'll do it," I exclaimed. This opportunity was a career-maker. "Thank you. I—I can't believe this."

"Good. You've earned it, Brielle. And you'll have New Year's Day off."

Good, because there'd be no way I could work the ball drop and make it to work again a couple of hours later.

"Coleman Gibbs will be here by the time the noon show wraps. We'll get some photos of the two of you for promotion."

I thought I was going to faint. *Coleman Gibbs. Emmy Award winning Coleman Gibbs. Coleman Gibbs who has his own freaking show for heaven's sake.*

I pulled myself together. "That sounds great. Thank you, Shelby. Thank you so much for this opportunity."

She nodded. "You're welcome. Now go get ready for your show. We'll talk more about it later."

I practically skipped out of her office.

Fatima touched me up as I went through the show notes before going on air. My whole mood had changed after my meeting with Shelby.

Fatima noticed. "Did you get your rainbow?"

I grinned. "Yes, I think I did."

I flicked the page up on my tablet and froze when I read the part about a fire on the Upper West Side that morning where two firemen had been trapped. There weren't any names and I fought the strong urge to pull out my phone and call Keith. I went so far as to unblock his number and type out a text asking if he was okay, but I never sent it. My good mood vanished and fear bubbled to the surface.

Fatima hit me with some powder. "You're all set."

In a daze, I migrated to my seat at the news desk. My legs shook. *Please let him be okay.* I didn't know what was worse knowing that Keith might be injured or caring about the fact that Keith might be injured.

SEVENTEEN

KEITH

Jace's frantic voice carried through the radio, "Mayday, mayday, mayday. Firefighters down. Ceiling collapse on the second floor. Hogan is pinned. Hart and the victim—status unknown."

The PASS alarm on my SCBA blared loudly. Whenever a firefighter stopped moving for more than thirty seconds, an alarm built into our breathing apparatus would sound. It was used to indicate the location of a downed firefighter. It could also be set off intentionally if you needed to alert others to your location. But I hadn't intentionally set mine off. No, I was immobile.

What the fuck happened? Everything was a bit fuzzy and I couldn't see shit. I groaned as I tried to get to my knees, but stopped as soon as I felt the body beneath me. The events that had transpired came rushing back. I rolled to my side, tossing debris off my back and deactivating my PASS alarm, then placed my hand on the woman's chest to see if it was rising. It wasn't. Shit, she'd stopped breathing. I tugged my glove off and the heat stung my skin as I felt her neck for a pulse.

Nothing.

I put my glove back on. "Dylan," I shouted. His PASS alarm was blaring over by the door and I prayed he was all right.

I warred with myself. The victim needed CPR imminently, otherwise, if she managed to survive, she'd be brain dead, but I also needed to get us out of there or we'd both be dead. The heat had magnified and even though I couldn't see it, I knew we were surrounded by fire.

I hit the button on my radio. "Mayday, mayday, mayday. This is Hart. I'm trapped with a victim in cardiac arrest."

I laced my fingers and started pumping on the woman's chest, feeling her ribs crack beneath the heel of my hand.

Jace replied, "It's going to take a while before we can get you out the door, Hart. It's blocked."

Fuck.

I continued chest compressions with one hand while I responded into my radio, "Get the aerial and a basket to the front window on the second floor." Then, I added, "Hogan?"

Relief swept over me when Dylan replied, "Here. My fucking leg is trapped."

I needed to help my brother, but leaving the victim wasn't an option. Since there was a floor above us, whatever had been in the room on the third floor over the collapse area had fallen down on top of us. Thankfully, the entire ceiling hadn't caved in, but it was severely compromised and was likely to give way at any second.

I continued to perform compressions and prayed like hell we'd make it out of there alive. The fact that I'd survived this far was a dang miracle, but that could change at any moment. I thought of Brielle and I promised God that if I made it, I would do everything in my power to track her down and get her back. If God blessed me with a second chance to live, I'd make her mine again—at any cost.

The sound of glass breaking to my left was like sweet music. Besides the fact that it would cause the fire to expand, that is. Frisco, one of the guys on my squad, came through the window with a Stokes basket.

"Over here," I called out. Frisco helped me strap the woman into the basket, then we scooted her to the window. Frisco got onto the ladder and we lifted the victim up onto it, then Frisco started to walk her down.

"I'm going back for Hogan," I announced.

"Hart, no. It's not safe."

I disregarded Frisco's orders and, ignoring the heat—adrenaline was one hell of a thing—I charged across the room, tossing furniture and debris aside as I neared the doorway. "Hogan, where are you?" I shouted.

Jace shouted back. "He's stuck under a dresser. I can't get to it from here and I don't want to climb on top of it and make things worse."

"I'll get it." I felt around for the dresser. When my fingers found the drawer pulls, I shouted, "Got it." I stretched my arms out and curled my fingers around the edges. "I'm gonna lift it on three. Jace, you pull Hogan out. One, two, three."

I grunted and my muscles strained as I lifted the solid wood piece about six inches.

"He's out," Jace shouted and I dropped the dresser.

The house rumbled again.

"Move," I screamed as I dove head first through the obstructed doorway. I landed on my stomach in the hall as the rest of the ceiling gave out and landed right where I'd been trapped with the victim.

"Hart?" Dylan screamed.

"I'm good." I got up on my knees. "Can you walk?"

"I think my fucking ankle's snapped."

Jace grabbed Dylan by the shoulders. "We've got you."

I grabbed his legs, taking care to avoid his ankle, and we bolted down the steps and out the front door. We got Dylan onto a stretcher and then I removed my helmet and whipped the mask off my face.

"You good, bro?" I patted Dylan's arm while Jace helped him get his mask off and the medics checked out his ankle.

"Yeah. Thanks."

"Don't sweat it."

His eyes locked with mine. "You should've gotten on that ladder. You didn't have to come back."

"You'd do the same for me."

Actually, he already had. Dylan had saved my ass on more than one occasion. At one point or another, we'd all needed rescuing.

They loaded him into the ambulance and I went over to Frisco. "How's the victim?"

"They're on the way to the hospital. Got her on a defibrillator and brought her back on scene."

I breathed out in relief. "That's good. Thanks for helping me out, man."

"You're a crazy motherfucker, Hart. Going back in there like that. You got damn lucky today."

I nodded. Almost *too* lucky. I hoped it was a sign of better things to come.

WE MADE it back to the firehouse just in time for the News at Noon. Being that it was Monday, this was the first chance I'd had to see Brielle since Kentucky, and I was grateful as hell I'd gotten back in time to see it. Relief flooded me when I saw her. Even though she'd told me she was safe, it killed me to not be able to verify that with my own eyes. I had no idea how she'd managed to beat me back from Kentucky, but

I'd been worried sick that something might've happened to her.

Her smile, which normally lit up her entire face, seemed forced and there was less enthusiasm in her voice than usual. My heart fluttered a little. If she was as miserable as I was, maybe I still had a chance. She was as beautiful as ever, though.

An image from the fire we'd been at popped up behind her head and she spoke into the camera, "A historic brownstone on the Upper West Side caught fire just after ten o'clock this morning, trapping two firefighters and a victim inside. Let's go to Katie Corelli who is on the scene. Katie." Her voice was shaky as hell and the worry was evident across her face.

Oh, Elle. I'm okay.

Overwhelmed with the desire to comfort her. I jogged to my locker to get my phone.

Keith: Saw your report. Yes, I was one of the guys who was trapped, but I'm okay. Promise. I'm finishing out my shift.
Keith: Also, you look beautiful.

I made my way back to the lounge to finish watching her show. If all I was going to get was half an hour of her every weekday through a television, I was going to savor every second. As the show ended, her co-host said, "You can catch us here every Monday through Friday for the News at Noon. But before we sign off, Brielle, I hear you'll be making an additional appearance this week."

She smiled. I loved that smile.

"Yes, this week I'll be co-hosting the USBC New Year's Eve Celebration alongside Coleman Gibbs directly from Times Square. Don't miss it."

That was my in. I couldn't get to her in the studio, but she wouldn't be able to miss me if I was standing front and center by the stage in Times Square on New Year's Eve. New Yorkers avoided midtown like the plague on New Year's Eve—it was strictly a tourist trap—but I would brave it for her. She was worth being trapped in a crowd for twelve hours in the cold. I'd pee in a dang bottle if I had to. Nothing was going to keep me away. Nothing.

EIGHTEEN

It was beyond surreal standing in the heated tent behind the stage in Times Square on New Year's Eve waiting to host the live show. While I had experience with anchoring long shows when I'd filled in for the morning show a few times, I doubted that would be anything like this. Not only would it be broadcast to millions of people across the country, I'd be on stage in front of thousands. Even my parents would be watching from London, where it was already the new year. They planned to stay up all night and watch me live.

Without a doubt, that night would be one of the highlights of my career. I'd met my co-host, Coleman, a few times, but we'd never worked together and I was rather intimidated. He was famous—and not just locally. I was eager to learn from him. I'd told him that a few days before when we'd met to discuss logistics, and I think he took my comment to heart because he had quickly stepped into a mentor role. I desperately wanted to impress him.

It was freezing that night. Temperatures had dipped into the teens and I was grateful for the heated tent. I didn't know how the crowd had survived being out there all day. Talk about dedication. I pulled the white faux-fur stole up over my shoulders. I had on a red wool coat with matching red wool pants. The outfit had been supplied by the designer in exchange for me mentioning them at some point during the show.

Very different from my little local news show, that's for sure. I wore my own clothes for that. This outfit was all kinds of fancy. I looked like Christmas.

Christmas...

Talk about a disaster. That whole weekend had been abysmal and Monday had been excruciating. I'd never been so glad to see a text from Keith before in my life. Finding out he was okay offered me some much-needed relief. I'd even texted him back saying I was glad to hear it. Then, I had promptly blocked him again because I'd known he'd want to try and talk and I'd been feeling weak, so I probably would've engaged with him, and nothing good would've come out of that. I was done falling for his game.

That afternoon, I'd moved all of my things to my parents' place, leaving Keith permanently behind me. Three days later, I was still trying to convince myself I'd done the right thing. These moments of weakness would creep in making me try to convince myself that I'd misunderstood and that Keith hadn't actually been setting me up to be used. Wishful thinking.

Coleman tapped me on the shoulder. "Ready?"

I forced a smile. "Absolutely."

I followed him to the tent exit and shook out my limbs trying to expel all thoughts of Keith. The producer gave us the cue and we walked over to the steps and went up onto the stage. Hands down the most surreal moment of my life. People were crowded between the barricades as far as I could see. The billboard lights illuminated the street and I glanced behind me to see the iconic Waterford crystal ball perched high in the air. The whole scene gave me chills.

I followed Coleman's lead and waved to the crowd. Their excitement was palpable and I laughed from the buzz of their cheers as we hit our marks on stage. The stage was carpeted and there were high chairs for us to sit in, dead center. They'd be moved out of the way when the musical artists performed.

Coleman started us off and the show flowed from there. By the third commercial break, I was feeling confident and energized by the thrill of hosting a show of that magnitude. But I was also cold. Very, very cold. So we dipped into the tent to warm up for a minute.

As we went back to the stage, something just behind the barrier caught the corner of my eye. Or rather I should say someone. Keith.

Surely, I had to be seeing things. Keith and I had spent New Year's Eves together before and he'd flat out said he'd never be caught dead in Times Square for the ball drop. Refusing to look again, I climbed the steps to the stage. My willpower lasted me all of ninety-seconds. While the network was airing coverage from one of our crowd reporters, I glanced to my left.

My eyes hadn't been betraying me. There he was—right up front—wearing his hunter green ski jacket and a gray knit hat. Keith never wore winter hats. He must've been freezing. I couldn't fathom how long he'd been out there to land a spot up front. He smiled and the hope in his eyes stung. I got teary and snapped my head away to gain control of myself. For once, I was grateful for the cold. That could explain the water in my eyes.

We left the stage again to make room for one of the musical artists and I fought back the desire to look at Keith. I couldn't believe he was there. Truly, it blew my mind. I didn't know how to feel about it.

Back on stage, I kept my eyes everywhere but where he was standing. We tossed to Macie, one of our crowd reporters, and I turned my back to Keith to look at the screen.

She said, "I'm here with a man who has a message for someone special. Tell us who you are and where you're from, sir."

"My name is Keith Hart and I live right here in Manhattan."

My whole body tensed and I spun to look at him in the crowd.

Macie commented, "Wow, we rarely see New Yorkers out here. What made you decide to spend New Year's Eve in Times Square?"

"My girl." He stared directly at me. "She left me and I need to get her back."

A hushed awe echoed through the crowd.

"That is so sweet," Macie gushed. "How does coming out here do that?"

"She's forced to hear me out this way."

"Then, the floor is yours."

He rubbed his lips together, then said, "I love you, Elle. I have for years and I never realized it. What you and I have is rare. Special. And I'm not giving up on us. I'll never give up on us."

A breath caught in my throat and I whimpered. Coleman noticed and glanced between me and Keith. Yeah, he'd figured it out. *Great, now I'm that girl.*

The crowd cheered for him and Macie said, "That is the sweetest thing. I hope you two get your happily ever after. Back to you, Coleman and Brielle."

I'd never had to snap myself together so quickly before.

Coleman, like a true professional, jumped right in and took my opening lines before going into his own to buy me a little time. I took a few breaths to compose myself before my next lines.

During the following commercial break, I raced into the tent and located my phone, which had been left in my purse with one of the producers. I pulled it out, unblocked Keith and sent him a text before I could talk myself out of it.

Brielle: Meet you at your apartment after the show? We can talk.

His response was almost immediate.

Keith: Yes. Absolutely. You're killing it up there tonight. I'm so proud of you.
Keith: And thank you.

My heart got all fluttery and my lips got all smiley and my stomach got all swoony. What Keith had done—putting himself out there like that in front of millions of people—must've been tough for him. Keith had never been one for the spotlight, yet he'd stepped directly into it...for me.

Confusion clouded my judgment. I couldn't believe he would do something like that if he'd simply been using me. It didn't make any sense.

Coleman appeared and put his hand on my shoulder. "You good."

I nodded. "Yeah. Thank you for covering. I really appreciate it."

"No problem. We should head back out."

"Right." I tucked my phone into my purse.

"And I know this isn't my place. But what your boyfriend just did took some serious balls. Don't discount that."

I grinned. "I won't."

The rest of the show went by in a blur. Keith stayed the whole time and after we counted down to midnight and the ball dropped, I looked over at him. He mouthed, *I love you*, and I had to bite my lip to keep from saying it back.

IT WAS NEARLY two in the morning by the time I knocked on Keith's door. I'd left my key with security after I'd moved out on Monday. Although, I wouldn't have used it if I'd kept it. Just getting to the door had taken every ounce of courage I had in me. The lock clicked back and I took a deep breath in preparation for being face-to-face with Keith.

"Elle." His smile sliced through my stoicism. He smelled of his musky bodywash and his hair was still wet. He made a t-shirt and sweatpants look damn good. Too good.

"Hi."

He stepped aside and I hesitated. I was having a weak moment and that was the last thing I needed for this conversation.

"Come on. I just want to talk," he coaxed.

He took my coat, revealing my sweatshirt and jeans, which was far less fancy than the borrowed outfit I'd worn all evening. I hadn't wanted to give it back.

I went inside and leaned against the kitchen island, not knowing what else to do with myself. It was weird being back in that apartment. I had loved every minute of living there and knowing it was no longer mine made me sad. Then I reminded myself that that part of my life had been one big lie.

"Thank you for coming over."

"I can't believe you spent all day in Times Square in this cold."

"Like I said, I'd do anything for you. I had to see you."

I crossed my arms over my chest.

He stood across from me, but kept his distance. "Can you tell me what made you leave?"

I rubbed my lips together. "I found out the truth."

"What truth?" He squinted.

"About you using me to help further your father's career."

His mouth fell open. "Excuse me?"

I exhaled loudly. "I heard you talking to your father about getting me pregnant so that he could have a black grandkid."

His hand flew up to cover his mouth. "You heard that?"

"Yeah. So needless to say, I'm done with being your family's token black girl. I don't appreciate being used. And I sure as hell don't appreciate you trying to get me pregnant to further your father's career."

He stepped forward. "I'm sorry, did you say you think I tried to get you pregnant?"

I couldn't believe he was seriously going to deny it. "Your plan didn't work. I took the morning after pill." Albeit, two days late because I'd forgotten, but it had worked, so I'd dodged that bullet, at least.

He put his palms together and touched the tips of his fingers to his lips. "Elle, I was never trying to get you pregnant. Honest-to-God, I genuinely forgot about the condom."

I scoffed. "Right. And then you just so happen to go from coming inside of me to a conversation with your dad about us having a baby."

He shook his head rapidly. "Clearly you didn't hear the whole conversation."

"No?" *How convenient.*

"No. Because after my father made that deeply offensive comment, I called him a racist son of a bitch, then told him to stay the hell away from us and that I was done with him and his politics."

I ran my tongue over my teeth. I desperately wanted to believe him, but I wasn't convinced. "I heard you *thank* him after he said what he did."

"Yeah, I thanked him for making my decision to cut myself off from him an easy one. Then I stormed out to look for you so we could come home, but you were gone." His voice cracked on that last part.

That sounded more like the Keith I knew. Something told me to believe him, but it was probably wishful thinking.

He stepped closer and reached for me, but I side-stepped him. Then he said, "Elle, I would never, *ever* use you—for any reason. I am not my father. I swear to you when I say I haven't spoken to him since and I have no intention of ever speaking to him again. I'm done. I'm out. He will never be able to use us for his own benefit. I promise you that. Please, baby, believe me."

Had I really gotten it all wrong?

KEITH

I was seething with anger, but tried to desperately hide it. I was pissed that she'd heard what my father had said. It had been hurtful enough for me to hear it and I sure as hell didn't want her to ever find out about it, let alone have heard it with her own ears. I'd never been more ashamed of my father in my life. And that was saying a lot.

There was also a part of me that was a little angry with her. How could she possibly believe that I'd ever do such a thing? But mostly, I was heartbroken because I could only imagine the pain she'd been in since that night—believing what she did.

I could never pretend to understand what it was like to be black, and I knew that by being with Brielle, we might face some ignorance in our lives together, but the life we could have would be worth it. Our love would always win. But first, I had to get Brielle to believe me.

She sighed heavily. "I don't know."

I swallowed the lump in my throat. No way in hell was I going to lose her over this. "You know me better than anyone.

Can you honestly tell me that you believe I could ever do something like that to you? To anyone?"

She uncrossed her arms and let her face fall forward into her hands. "No, but...I heard you, Keith. And I don't know what to believe anymore."

I had to touch her, so I placed my hands around her biceps and she looked up at me with watery eyes. "Yes, you do. You know it in your heart. Just like I do. I love you with everything that I am, Elle. *You* are my family now. Tell me what you need me to do to prove that to you."

Her face pinched and it killed me to see so much anguish in her expression. She bit her lip. "I need to tell you about Mitchell."

Well, that was unexpected. I dropped my hands. "Who's Mitchell?"

She sat down in one of the bar chairs at the island, while I stayed put. "He was my boyfriend—my *white* boyfriend. He had political dreams and his sights were set on a job in the mayor's office. The black mayor."

Dang. I knew where that story was going.

"He used me to get himself that job. Obviously, I ended it when I found out, but I promised myself I'd never let someone use me like that again."

I sighed. "And then you met my parents."

She nodded.

I'd never been more ashamed of my family than I had that past month. Their behavior toward Brielle had been inexcusable. I'd spoken to Corbett and he'd told me that they couldn't understand why what my father had said was wrong. My brother understood, though, and he got the head of my father's PR team to sign him up for sensitivity training. I sure as hell hoped he'd take it seriously. If there was ever a chance of us reconciling, they'd have to make some major changes.

I sighed. "So you're struggling to believe me because Mitchell had tricked you into believing he cared for his own gain?"

She nodded again.

I rubbed my hand over the stubble on my chin. "He's a scumbag and I'm sorry he did that to you. I will gladly knock him out if I ever meet him, but I'm *not* him. You know me. We've been friends for years."

"I know."

I shook my head. "I've learned a lot over this past month. Not only from my parents' reprehensible behavior, but also from your mom and dad. They're what family should be." I stared down at my feet. "I don't need my parents in my life anymore because I can create my own family. A family with you."

I hated what had to happen next, but I did it anyway. "I realize there's nothing I can say to prove I wasn't playing you. It's something you're going to have to figure out for yourself." I went over to the Christmas tree and removed the Rockette ornament and picked up a present from under the tree, then went back and placed both on the island in front of her. "You can trust me, Elle. Deep down you know you can, but I'm going to give you the space you need to figure that out." I pointed to the ornament. "But take that with you. I want you to remember *that*. Remember who we are as a couple. Hell, remember who we are as friends. Take your time and whenever you're ready, I'll be here."

She chewed her lip.

"You can open the present, too."

Her fingers ran along the glossy red paper a few times before she flipped it over to slide her finger into the seam. After removing the paper, she held the white box in her hands and took a few breaths before removing the cover.

She smiled. "You remembered?"

Inside were two tickets to *Wicked* on Broadway for later that month. She'd mentioned how the book had been one of her childhood favorites, but she'd never had a chance to see the show.

I nodded. "I know how much you want to see it." I swallowed. "Of course, I'd love to go with you, but if you want to take someone else, that's fine. As long as you get to experience it."

She blinked away tears. "Thank you."

I went into the kitchen, opened the junk drawer and pulled out her key, the one she'd left with the front desk, then I placed it next to the ornament. "You can come home whenever you want."

I'd just gotten her close to me again, yet there I was sending her away. It hurt all over.

She stood up and retrieved the ornament and her key, which made me hopeful. "I'll think about it."

And then she left.

IF I'D GOTTEN an hour of sleep that was a lot. Letting Brielle go the night before had been brutal. I sat on the couch drinking a mug of the tea that she'd left behind. It was chamomile and normally made me tired, which was the opposite of what I should be drinking at that moment, but it made me feel close to her.

I wanted her back more than anything and all I could do was wait and pray that she'd believe what I'd said. I couldn't blame her for having her doubts, but I hoped like hell that she'd be able to push past the hurt and realize the truth.

I didn't have to work until the next morning, so I laid out on the couch and wallowed in my sorrows. At some point, I must've fallen asleep because I was startled awake when I heard the door knob turn.

I hopped to my feet just in time to see Brielle walk in. With a suitcase in hand.

I ran to her. "Does this mean...?"

She nodded. "I'd like to come home."

I wrapped my arms around her and lifted her straight into the air. "Baby, you have no idea how happy that makes me." I put her back down and cupped her face. "I've missed you so much."

She grinned. "I've missed you, too. I'm sorry."

I furrowed my brows. "Don't be. I don't blame you for a second. I'm sorry that my family hurt you."

Her fingers brushed against my cheek. "I'm sorry they hurt you, too. You deserve better."

"We'll never have to worry about them again. I promise you."

She nodded. "Did you really mean what you said last night about me being your family?"

I smiled. "Every word."

"I like that."

And then I kissed her. It was a kiss to beat all others because this kiss meant so much more. With my lips, I promised to always put her first. We were a team and I'd have her back no matter what.

I slid my fingers over her cheek as I promised to treasure her and love her the way she deserved to be loved.

I dropped a hand to her lower back and tugged her against me, promising to protect her at all costs.

By the time we broke the kiss, we both had tears in our eyes.

She smiled. "I love you, too, Keith. Always will."

And I kissed her again.

EPILOGUE – ONE YEAR LATER

Keith

I was determined to make this Christmas so amazing that it'd erase all memory of our last Christmas. Once Brielle had moved back in, we'd picked up right where we'd left off. The only difference was, I started telling her I loved her pretty much all day, every day. I'd never tire of saying those words, or hearing her say them back.

I sat by our Christmas tree—which we'd cut down ourselves, again—with my arm around Brielle while we sipped on a glass of wine and waited for her parents to arrive. They were spending Christmas at our apartment with us. As we sat in silence, I reflected on everything we'd gone through in our relationship.

It had been one hell of a year.

Brielle had gotten an anchor spot on the USBC Morning News after one of the anchors took a job in D.C., leaving an opening. We both wondered if my parents had anything to do with it, but since I hadn't spoken to them, we'd never know.

Probably better that way. The Colonel was officially running for President and Corbett was busy as hell with the campaign.

Blair had given birth to my niece in May and she and Corbett had even come to visit us in New York a couple of times. At least he and I had been able to salvage our relationship and he never pushed me to patch things up with our parents. Although, he had told me they'd finally admitted to being in the wrong. Step in the right direction.

There was a knock on the door and Brielle got up to get it. I placed my wine on the coffee table and stood so I could greet her parents. They pulled Brielle in for hugs and I went to the door to help them with their coats.

Kim wrapped her arms around me. "Keith, it's so good to see you. Thank you for having us for Christmas."

"Of course. We're so glad that you could make it."

Her dad hugged me next, pulling me in tight. "Merry Christmas, son."

"Merry Christmas, Douglas. Come in let me take your coats." I hung them up in the front closet.

Brielle followed her parents into the living room while I went to the kitchen to get them drinks. I poured a scotch for her dad and a glass of wine for her mom, then joined them in the living room by the tree.

I'd grown close with her parents over the past year. As promised, her father had visited me at the firehouse—more than once—and it made me realize how badly I'd needed that kind of fatherly support. Douglas stepped right in and filled that role without hesitation.

As for Kim, she was the sweetest woman I'd ever had the pleasure of knowing. Brielle had clearly gotten her mother's heart of gold. The last time we'd had dinner at their house, Kim had told us she'd be retiring after next year. She was getting tired of traveling and she wanted to spend more time with her husband and her daughter. Brielle had been ecstatic to hear it.

As far as in-laws went, I'd won the lottery. But I'm getting ahead of myself.

Right after Thanksgiving, I'd gone out to Long Island, while Brielle was at a holiday party at work, and I'd had dinner with her parents. Call me traditional, but I didn't feel right asking Brielle to marry me without their blessing. They'd both given it to me. Kim had cried and Douglas had bought us a bottle of champagne to celebrate.

I'd known from the beginning Brielle and I would get married one day. My feelings for her were too strong for our relationship to be anything less than forever. Her mom had gone shopping with me in the city earlier that month to pick out a ring, which ended up being a much more daunting task than I'd anticipated. Then Kim had an idea that was nothing short of brilliant. I'd ended up having something custom made and I couldn't wait for Brielle to see it. I'd picked it up earlier that week and it was absolutely perfect.

My plan was for us to have dinner, which I admit I had catered because I didn't want Brielle to have to work in the kitchen and obviously I couldn't cook, and then we were going to open presents and I would propose. But I was impatient, even more-so since her parents had arrived, so I decided to screw the plan and just go for it.

Brielle was talking about her work on the New Jersey Gang Violence Prevention Task Force and I didn't want to interrupt her, but the words came out of my mouth anyway. I was too excited.

"Baby, I want to give you a present."

She cocked her head at me. I never interrupted her so rudely. "Now? I thought we were going to wait until after dinner."

"I know, but there's one that I really want you to have now."
I took her wine glass from her and put it on the table with mine.
"Umm, okay."
I went under the tree and pulled out the box, which was wrapped in a metallic blue paper and tied with a white bow so it matched our tree. Then I handed it to her and sat back on the couch beside her. My leg wouldn't stop shaking as she took her time unwrapping it.

It was a sterling silver ornament shaped like a present and it had our names and the year engraved on it. She smiled at me. "Thank you. It's perfect for our collection." We'd started collecting ornaments from all of the cool places we'd gone together.

My heart pounded. "There's more. It opens."
Her thumb flicked open the clasp and she lifted the lid revealing the diamond ring. She gasped and her hand flew up to cover her mouth.

I got down on one knee. "Elle, you're my best friend. You're my family. You're my today, my tomorrow, my everything." I swallowed the emotion in my throat. "Will you marry me?"

Her eyes welled up with tears and the biggest smile stretched across her face. "Yes, of course."

My shaking hands reached for the ring and I pulled it from the box and put it on her finger. She dropped the ornament as I wrapped my arms around her and held her tight.

Her parents clapped and joined our hug. The four of us cried happy tears. Our family was becoming official. Then, Kim broke out the champagne and we celebrated.

Brielle couldn't stop staring at her hand.
"Do you like it?" I asked.
"I love it."
"There's something else you need to know." I pointed to the

pear-shaped diamond at the center of the halo on the rose gold band. "The center stone was your grandmother's."

Her lip trembled and she looked over at her parents. "From Nan's ring?"

They both nodded and her dad said, "She wanted you to have it, bunny."

Brielle sniffled. "Thank you. It—it's perfect. Absolutely perfect."

I kissed her forehead and held her close. Brielle was going to be my wife and I couldn't ask for anything more out of this life. In her, I had everything I'd ever need.

Once her parents left later that night, she sat beside me on the couch and I held her to my side while she stared at the sparkly new addition to her finger.

"I love you, Keith." She nuzzled her head against my chest.

"I love you, too. So much."

"Thank you."

"What for?" I asked.

"For making this the best Christmas ever."

I grinned. "I should be thanking you. All I did was ask. You're the one who said yes and made it official."

She turned her face toward me. "Kiss me."

My lips touched hers and I knew that no matter what life decided to throw at us, we'd always make it through as long as we had each other.

She pulled away and smiled. "Merry Christmas."

I smiled back. "Merry Christmas, baby."

BONUSES

Want Bonus Content from Keith and Brielle?
Get it now for free by going to
www.kayekennedy.com/brielle

Help others fall in love with Keith and Brielle by leaving a
review on Amazon, GoodReads, and BookBub.

Want more of my firefighter world?
It all starts with *Burning for More*

He's reckless. She's hiding behind a lie. They seem destined to
be, but could easily crash and burn. Dylan might be the savior
that Autumn never knew she needed, but first, she'll have to
save him from himself. Find out if love conquers all in this sexy
romance with a twist that'll take your breath away!

You can interact with me, chat all things romance, and get access to freebies in my exclusive **Facebook Group Romance Reads that Kiss & Tell**

Join my Romance Readers Club and be the first to find out about new releases and giveaways! You'll also get free bonus scenes and fun extras.

Sign up at www.kayekennedy.com

WHAT TO READ NEXT

WANT TO STAY IN THE HOLIDAY SPIRIT?

Merry Ex-Mas is a standalone set in a picturesque small town in the Adirondack Mountains. If you wish Hallmark had an open-door policy, then this steamy romance will be your jam!

When a burnt-out attorney escapes the city's chaos for a hometown holiday, she stumbles upon a lot more than snow-covered streets

At the eleventh hour, I made the impulsive decision to close my laptop and drive upstate to my tiny hometown of Evergreen Falls, NY and surprise my family for Christmas.

I never imagined I'd get stuck in a blizzard and run off the road by a deer. Even more unexpected, was that my ex-boyfriend would be the one to rescue me from the ditch.

We didn't exactly end on good terms ten years ago, now we're snowed in at a bed and breakfast in the middle of nowhere, with no internet or cell service, sharing the only vacant room.

This Ex-Mas might just change everything...

P.S. If you plan on taking a holiday road trip in the mountains, always check the weather.

P.P.S. On second thought, don't.

Will a little small-town holiday magic melt the barriers around the heart of this big-city lawyer? Or will the frostbite of the past be too much to overcome?

Gilmore Girls meets *Hart of Dixie* in this heartwarming holiday romance between a small-town single dad and a curvy big-city lawyer.

Read Now
www.books2read.com/merry-ex-mas

ACKNOWLEDGMENTS

Without the following individuals, this story may never have been told:

- My fairy godmothers for always believing in me and for being proof that you can pick your family.
- My grandmother for fostering my love of reading from a young age and for always being my number one fan—no matter what I do.
- Sam, who is the best idea sounding board there is. He had to talk me off the ledge a few times with this one.
- August Head of Walter's Writing Emporium for guiding me to make this story the best it could be and for working faster than seemingly possible to keep me on deadline.
- My sensitivity readers for making sure I honored this story in the best way possible
- Jaycee DeLorenzo for bringing my vision for the cover to life.
- My street team for being awesome and for loving Keith and Brielle as much as I do
- YOU for taking a chance on love with my characters

<u>Small Town Holiday Standalones</u>

Merry Ex-Mas

Pumpkin Spice & Prophecies

Not My Valentine

<u>Burning for the Bravest Series</u>

If you like alpha males with soft centers who love hard and make love harder, then this series featuring New York City firefighters is for you!

Burning for More – Dylan & Autumn

Burning for This – Jesse & Lana

Burning for Her – Ryan & Zoe

Burning for Fate – Jace & Britt

Burning for You – Kyle & Allie

Burning for You: The Wedding – Kyle & Allie

Burning for Love – Declan & Gwen

Burning for Trouble – Mack & Tori

Burning for Secrets - Brix & Georgia

Burning for Reality - Theo & Kenzie

Burning for Christmas - Keith & Brielle

<u>Flirting with the Finest Series</u>

Follow the men and women of the Special Investigations Task Force in New York City as they fight crime and fall in love.

Flirting with Forever – Hunter & Lauren

Flirting with Fame - Tai & Bellamy

Flirting with Faith - Erik & Aubrey

Flirting with Freedom - Cooper & Leila

<u>**Rescued by the Rangers Series**</u>

Follow a team of former Army Rangers turned independent contractors who've taken on the most challenging missions, but have struggled to find love. Until now.

Rescuing Griffin - Free Prequel to Book 1

http://www.kayekennedy.com/rbc-prequel

Rescued by Chance – Griffin & Holly

Rescued by Loyalty — Nick & Mia

ABOUT THE AUTHOR

Kaye Kennedy is the author of contemporary romance and romantic suspense novels featuring everyday heroes who love hard and make love harder. Fun fact: she used to be a firefighter and now she writes about them! If you like steamy and soulful reads that will break your heart and put it back together again, then her stories are for you. In her books, you can always expect a happily ever after that kisses and tells.

She earned her degree in English Literature and taught college composition & literature classes before switching gears entirely and becoming an entrepreneur, starting multiple businesses. In addition to writing, Kaye sees clients as a psychic medium and serves as a coach for authors wanting to level up their careers.

While originally from New York, Kaye has lived in New

Hampshire and Florida, but now calls Connecticut home. She is battling an invisible illness and resides with her rescue mutt turned service dog, Zeus, who is a character in Burning for Secrets. Kaye's real-life HEA is her favorite trope: friends-to-lovers (and will one day be turned into a book). When she isn't writing, she's out paddling on the water, indulging in a beach read, checking out a brewery, or feeding her wanderlust.

You can interact with Kaye and get access to freebies in her exclusive Facebook Group: Romance Reads that Kiss & Tell. If you really want to be entertained, check her out on TikTok @authorkayekennedy.

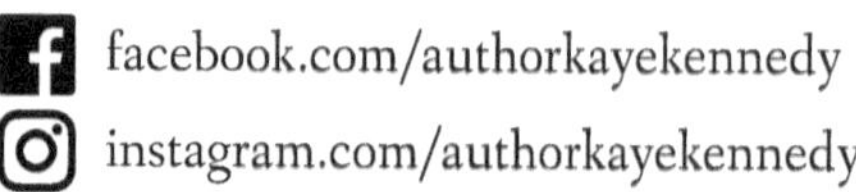

facebook.com/authorkayekennedy

instagram.com/authorkayekennedy